Twins Reuni

A very [illegible]

Pediatric consultant Josh Stanmore can—quite literally!—not believe his eyes when he finds himself face-to-face with Gloucester General Hospital's newest doctor, Lachlan McKendry. It's like looking in a mirror! As Josh and Lachlan's working lives entwine on the children's ward, they start to unravel the secrets of their past… But it's the help of two inspirational women that will let them look to a future that they never thought possible!

Meet Josh and Lachlan in…

A Pup to Rescue Their Hearts

Josh Stanmore thought his life was complete… until pup Lucky and single mom Stevie step into his life—and leave his heart wanting more!

A Surgeon with a Secret

Surgeon Lachlan's life is falling apart… Can nurse Flick be the one to help him put it back together?

Dear Reader,

I'd like to introduce to you Josh Stanmore and Lachlan McKendry. They were separated at birth and adopted into very different families—one ordinary and one of extreme wealth and privilege. One knows he's adopted, but one has never been told. They had different reasons to choose a career in medicine, but they've both ended up in the pediatric field, which is how they unexpectedly meet each other. They have different reasons to mistrust family and love, but they're both about to take on what could be the biggest challenge of their lives—finding love…

Josh and Lachlan are extraordinary men and they both needed absolutely amazing women. Come and meet Stevie and Flick. I hope that you'll love them as much as I do!

Happy reading!

With love,

Alison Roberts
xx

A PUP TO RESCUE
THEIR HEARTS

———

ALISON ROBERTS

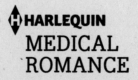

HARLEQUIN

MEDICAL
ROMANCE

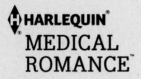

HARLEQUIN®
MEDICAL
ROMANCE™

Recycling programs
for this product may
not exist in your area.

ISBN-13: 978-1-335-40428-2

A Pup to Rescue Their Hearts

Alison Roberts is a New Zealander, currently lucky enough to be living in the South of France. She is also lucky enough to write for the Harlequin Medical Romance line. A primary school teacher in a former life, she is now a qualified paramedic. She loves to travel and dance, drink champagne, and spend time with her daughter and her friends.

Books by Alison Roberts

Harlequin Medical Romance

Royal Christmas at Seattle General
Falling for the Secret Prince

Medics, Sisters, Brides
Awakening the Shy Nurse
Saved by Their Miracle Baby

Rescue Docs
Resisting Her Rescue Doc
Pregnant with Her Best Friend's Baby
Dr. Right for the Single Mom

Hope Children's Hospital
Their Newborn Baby Gift

Twins on Her Doorstep
Melting the Trauma Doc's Heart
Single Dad in Her Stocking
The Paramedic's Unexpected Hero

Visit the Author Profile page
at Harlequin.com for more titles.

CHAPTER ONE

PAUSING ON HIS way to grab a coffee in the paediatric ward's staffroom was a deliberate action on the part of Dr Josh Stanmore. He'd spotted that new nurse coming towards him and, as Head of Department, he knew it was high time he introduced himself and made this new staff member feel welcome. He'd noticed her before, of course. Who wouldn't when that wildly curly, rich auburn hair would make her stand out in any crowd? The fact that she was undeniably gorgeous was not something that was consciously crossing Josh's mind right then, however. His motive was professional, not personal.

Even more unlikely to occur to him was the thought that this momentary, random interruption, in his quest to find a caffeine hit to help get him through the rest of a busy afternoon, would end up saving a life.

Maybe it was because he didn't want the newest addition to the paediatric staff of Gloucester General Hospital to feel intimidated by the HOD watching her approach that made him avert his gaze for a moment. To turn his head and glance through the windows of the playroom that ran the width of this end of the ward. A playroom that was deserted for the moment because afternoon visiting hours were over and it was a rest time for all their patients.

Except…the playroom wasn't quite deserted, was it? Josh could see small, bare legs beside a large, pink bean bag. And an even smaller hand, lying palm upwards, with the fingers curled as if the child was asleep.

Or…unconscious?

With a muttered oath, Josh stepped swiftly through the door of the brightly decorated room, moving far enough to be able to see the rest of the child and instantly recognising that she wasn't one of the patients on this ward. This little girl wasn't wearing a plastic identification bracelet on her wrist and she was not wearing pyjamas or slippers. She had sparkly pink shoes on and a dark blue dress that was…*good grief*…almost the same shade as her lips.

It took Josh only another two strides before he could crouch beside the child. To check her mouth for any obvious obstruction to her airway and then slide his fingers down to her neck to feel for a pulse at the same time as assessing whether she was breathing or not.

She wasn't.

Josh had no idea how long this child had been unconscious. She wasn't breathing but she still had a palpable pulse so he wasn't too late. There was no time to go looking for equipment like a bag mask or a defibrillator. There was only one thing to do and Josh didn't hesitate. He pinched the little girl's nose shut as he pulled in some air before covering her mouth with his own to try and deliver a lifesaving breath. And then another.

Breaths that failed to make that small chest rise.

He knew he had to call for assistance but fear was enough to make him take another few seconds to scoop this little girl into his arms and turn her face down with her head lower than her chest. He flattened his hand so that he could apply back blows that might be effective enough to dislodge whatever was blocking her airway.

* * *

She'd seen him standing near the door to the playroom and the fact that her path was about to cross for the first time with that of the man who was effectively her new boss had been enough to make Stephanie Hawksbury's heart skip a beat. For a moment she thought he might be waiting for her but then he ducked into the playroom and, by the time she got close enough to see through the windows, he was on his knees on the floor, playing with a child.

Wait…

Nobody played with a child by hitting them on the back like that. It took Stevie only another split second to process what was actually going on and the armload of toys she'd been returning to the playroom fell from her arms to scatter and bounce on the floor. She shoved the door open, dragging in a deep breath.

'What do you need me to do, Doctor?'

'Get the door.' His words were terse as he got to his feet with the child cradled in his arms. 'Treatment room…*stat*…'

Stevie held the door and then ran to get in front of him so that she could hold the door of the well-equipped treatment room that was used for a wide range of procedures that included anything from inserting a new intravenous line to a full-on resuscitation attempt.

Like this one…

Josh Stanmore laid the small girl on the bed in the centre of the room. Stevie was already pushing the airway trolley closer. If he'd been delivering back blows, it was obvious that Josh thought this small patient was choking and it was very obvious that she was becoming hypoxic from lack of oxygen. The small face was as white as a sheet, making the contrast with her blue lips all the more shocking.

Stevie would get the defibrillator next, of course, because if the breathing had stopped completely, a cardiac arrest would not be far away. She also turned her head towards the large red button beside the door that could trigger a cardiac arrest alarm that would have a dedicated team rushing towards them to assist.

Josh must have seen the direction of her glance but he wasn't about to stop for anything just yet—perhaps because he knew he had all the equipment he needed in this room and that he also knew they had only a matter of minutes before irreversible brain damage could occur and they couldn't afford to lose even precious seconds. He didn't have a whole team of medics to direct but the intensity of the gaze that was currently fixed on Stevie suggested that he thought she was capable of providing whatever assistance he needed.

And, dammit…that was exactly what she going to do. Whatever it took. There was no way she was going to let a child die in front of her like this.

'Start chest thrusts,' Josh ordered. 'I'm going to try direct vision to see the obstruction. If that doesn't work, we're going to need to do a surgical airway.'

Stevie positioned one hand on the centre of the child's chest and began pushing in the same way she would for compressions in CPR. Even if the child's heart was still beating, this was the protocol for a choking child because the action, like back blows, could potentially dislodge the obstruction.

From the corner of her eye, she saw Josh choosing a curved blade to snap onto the handle of the laryngoscope and clicking on the light to test it. He was also scanning the trolley.

'I can't see any Magill's forceps.'

'Second drawer down on the left.'

'Got it.'

'Shall I try another breath?'

'Yep.'

Josh was at the head of the bed and was pulling the stainless-steel trolley close. As Stevie positioned the mask over the child's mouth and nose and squeezed the bag to try and deliver air to her lungs, she saw Josh tug the tie loose on a sterile pack and roll it out to open it.

A cricothyroidotomy kit, with a large IV cannula, five-mil syringe, oxygen tubing and a three-way stopcock for a needle cricothyroidotomy. There were also scalpels and tubing if a far more invasive surgical airway was required. Stevie's heart sank at both the glint of the scalpel and what her fingers were telling her as they tried to squeeze the bag. The air inside it was going nowhere.

'Still obstructed?'

'Yes.'

'Right…' Josh sounded perfectly calm. 'Let's see what's going on, shall we?'

He slid a rolled-up towel beneath the girl's shoulders to tilt her head into what was known as the 'sniffing' position. Holding the laryngoscope in his left hand, he gently inserted the blade into the right side of their patient's mouth and Stevie knew he would be displacing the tongue to the left, which could allow the bright light to show him any visible foreign body in her airway. His movements were careful and confident and, although she was holding her breath, Stevie realised she had complete faith in this doctor. He knew exactly what he was doing and he didn't appear to be at all intimidated by the fact that he was dealing with a life-or-death emergency and a ticking clock.

And he could see something... Stevie could only see the back of Josh's head but she could feel the intent focus of his entire body as he lifted the small-sized Magill's forceps he was holding in his right hand. Like an elongated and angled pair of scissors with blunt, circular ends, these forceps were specifically designed to be used in airways, to guide the placement of tubes or to remove foreign objects.

It was a delicate manoeuvre. Josh had tilted his head to be able to see what he was doing with the forceps and there was nothing Stevie could do for the moment other than watch. She saw the lines deepening around Josh's eyes that told her this was no easy task. She heard the tiny sigh that suggested relief as he seemed to be winning and then she noticed the way he caught the corner of his bottom lip between his teeth as he held onto his concentration.

And then his breath came out in a growl of frustration.

'Lost it,' he muttered. 'It's so slippery…'

Stevie swallowed hard. The next step would be to insert a needle into this child's neck, which would buy them a little more time, but if that didn't work, they would have to create a way to get air into her lungs by cutting a larger hole. And the seconds were ticking past relentlessly. Had she made a mistake in not hitting the alarm button sooner?

As if he'd heard her thought, Josh flicked her an upward glance.

'This time,' he said quietly. 'Trust me— we've got this.'

She did trust him, Stevie thought. Even though she didn't know this man at all— hadn't even been properly introduced to him, in fact, in the few days since she'd started working here—she was ready to trust him even when it was a child's life hanging in the balance.

He moved even more carefully this time

as he slipped the forceps down the little girl's throat, and the tension ramping up as he paused for a long moment to make sure he had a good grip on whatever the slippery object was, meant that Stevie could actually hear her own heartbeat thumping in her ears as she continued to hold her own breath.

It probably only took a few seconds for Josh to pull the forceps slowly clear but it felt like for ever because she had to know that they hadn't lost their grip. Relief surged through her body as she saw them emerge from the child's mouth with something between the ends and—in the same instant—she could see and hear the desperate gasp as the little girl sucked in her first breath in too long. Or had that sound come from her own lips and that was why Josh's glance flicked up again to meet hers?

If it was, he clearly understood. He held her gaze for no more than a heartbeat but she could see the relief in his own eyes and it was so genuine—and caring—that Stevie knew that this doctor was a person she could have the utmost respect for. That he was as trustworthy as her instincts had already decided. And that she liked him.

A lot.

'Let's get some oxygen on,' he said. 'I'm just going to have another look and make sure there's nothing else down there that I can see.'

'What was it?' Stevie looked at the sterile cloth on the trolley as she reached up to connect tubing to the overhead oxygen supply. 'Oh…a grape?'

'Yeah…' Josh was shining the light of his laryngoscope down the child's throat again. 'The message that you have to cut grapes for littlies still hasn't got out there well enough. I heard recently they're the third most common cause of food-related choking deaths in children. I can't see anything else down there.' He removed the blade of the laryngoscope, unhooked his stethoscope from around his neck and frowned as he focused on the small girl's face while fitting the earpieces. 'Who is she, do you know?'

Stevie shook her head. 'I'm guessing she's a sibling of one of our patients. She probably came in during visiting hours.'

She held the mask, now with oxygen running, over the girl's mouth and nose. Josh's hand brushed her arm as he moved the disc of the stethoscope to listen to their patient's chest. Stevie could feel the twitch of movement under the mask she was holding in place.

'I think she's waking up...'

'Good...'

Stevie knew why there was still a note of caution in Josh's tone. The girl was breathing on her own but would she regain consciousness fully? Had she been without adequate oxygenation long enough for brain damage to have occurred?

They both turned their heads as the door of the treatment room opened. It was the first time that Stevie had seen the paediatric ward's nurse manager, Ruby, without a smile on her face.

'What's happening, Josh? What do you need?'

'We're under control, thanks, Ruby. I found this girl unconscious in the playroom—respiratory arrest due to a totally obstructed airway.'

'Oh, dear Lord...' Ruby closed her eyes in a long blink. 'I was just helping with the hunt for Amelia here. Her baby brother has come in for observation and her mother was feeding him while the registrar did the admission. Dad went to the cafeteria to find a late lunch for them all and Mum assumed that Amelia had gone with him. It's panic stations out there. I'll have to let them know where she is.'

Ruby moved far more swiftly back to the door than Stevie would have expected for a woman of her size and age and she'd no more than poked her head into the corridor to call out to someone than she was stepping aside to let other people into the room.

A young man, who was holding a baby. And a terrified-looking young woman with a pale tear-streaked face.

'Oh, my God...' she sobbed. *Amelia...*'

The woman rushed towards the bed and, as she reached to touch her daughter, the little girl opened her eyes and burst into tears.

'Mumma...'

Stevie could feel the prickle of tears behind her own eyes. Happy tears, because the fact that Amelia was awake and speaking and knew who her mother was made it more than likely she had come through this life-threatening incident unscathed. It seemed the most natural thing in the world to look up and meet Josh's gaze yet again and, this time, it felt like an acknowledgement of a bond. The two of them had been the only people to share that very real fear, the tension of the fight, the relief of a successful outcome and now the joy of the world righting itself at least in this moment of time. A whole story that had taken only a couple of minutes but would be one that Stevie was never going to forget.

And, judging by the look in Dr Stanmore's eyes, he wasn't about to forget it, either.

'It's okay,' he reassured the crying mother. 'Amelia here choked on a grape but we were lucky enough to find her in time.'

Amelia was in her mother's arms now. 'Oh, thank you, Doctor. I can't thank you enough…you and…?' She looked over her daughter's head, her eyebrows raised.

'Stephanie, isn't it?' Josh was smiling. 'I need to thank you as well.'

Oh, man…the warmth in those dark eyes was enough to be making something melt somewhere in the middle of Stevie's chest.

'I get called Stevie,' she told him. She tried to return his smile but she had a horrible feeling that, in the emotional aftermath of a crisis averted, her lips might be too wobbly to cooperate so she broke the eye contact to turn back to Amelia and her mother. 'I'm sure I'll see you both again very soon.' She stepped back, knowing that she was no longer needed in here and that she had a lot of duties to catch up on now.

'We'll need to keep Amelia with us for a little while,' Josh added. 'Ruby, could you sort an urgent consult with someone from ENT, please? It's just a precaution,' he told Amelia's mother. 'But I wouldn't be surprised if she's got a bit of a sore throat now.'

'But what happened? What did you say she choked on?'

Stevie held the door for Ruby and they both slipped out of the room while Josh filled the parents in on the details of the incident.

'We'll have to do a detailed report on this,' Ruby told Stevie. 'I need to get this consult organised right now but could you come and see me in the office before your shift finishes, please?'

'Of course. I'll be there as soon as I can. I'm running a bit behind with obs on my patients now, though.'

'Emergencies tend to do that.' But Ruby was smiling. 'But well done, Stevie. I had a feeling the first day I met you that you were going to be an asset around here.'

Ruby's praise was as welcome as the warmth of Josh Stanmore's thanks had been and Stevie tackled the list of tasks associated with the four patients under her care on this shift with a growing confidence that her life was on a new track. A much, much better one than she'd been on for the last twelve years or so.

If only…

Between feeding and changing a baby whose mother had had to go home to her other children this afternoon, and taking a full set of observations, including an ECG on a four-year-old boy who had congenital heart disease currently complicated by a respiratory infection, Stevie snatched a moment to send a text.

Hey, Mattie…you home yet? Hope you had a better day at school xx

Thanks to one of the less pleasant duties of the day, getting a parent and a junior nurse to hold a wriggling, terrified toddler while Stevie got a blood sample, it was another half an hour before she noticed that her text had gone unanswered. It didn't surprise her but it did increase the background level of tension, especially as it would be another couple of hours before she could get home and see for herself that the other half of her life—the personal and most important half—was at least getting closer to stepping on the same track as her professional one.

She had a horrible feeling that it wasn't…

'Stevie…'

She dropped the test tube she'd just finished labelling into a plastic bag and began pressing the seal together, turning at the sound of her name. This time she managed to find a smile for the paediatric consultant who was, by all accounts, not only the most important doctor but the most popular man in this hospital department.

'Hi, Dr Stanmore. How's Amelia?'

'Call me Josh,' he said, propping his elbow on the higher shelf in front of the reception desk. 'And Amelia's fine. She's been cleared by ENT and gone home with her dad, who's got instructions to bring her back if he has any worries about her coughing or with any change in her breathing or swallowing.'

'Oh, that's so good to hear.' Stevie's smile widened.

'I just wanted to thank you again.' Josh was watching Stevie's hands as she folded the lab test request to put into the pocket on the side of the plastic bag. 'I couldn't have dealt with that emergency without the kind of calm, experienced assistance you were able to provide.'

The glow of pride was giving Stevie that melting sensation again and, as her gaze lifted to meet a pair of eyes that were dark enough to make it difficult to distinguish the pupil, she could feel something else contributing to that tingling in her gut. Attraction was the last thing she'd expected—or wanted—to ambush her like this but there was no mistaking that shaft of whatever it was a mixture of. Desire? Anticipation? Longing? *Hope...?*

'So...' Josh's smile was a bit lopsided now and one eyebrow had moved closer to the tumble of rather charmingly unkempt hair that was almost as curly as her own. 'I owe you a drink. What are you doing after work?'

'Sorry?' Stevie could feel her smile fading. That internal fizzing sensation was fading even faster.

'After work? Can I buy you a drink?' Josh's smile had also disappeared and that raised eyebrow now made him look a little puzzled. 'Doesn't have to be a wine. How 'bout a coffee?'

'You're...asking me out? For a drink?' Stevie spoke carefully. Slowly enunciating each syllable, which was the complete opposite of the way her brain was firing very rapid messages. Images of another attractive man. Another paediatric consultant, in fact. Echoes of a day that had changed her life for ever.

'Come for a drink with me, after work. And I'm not going to take "no" as an answer...'

'Just to say thanks for your help today.' Josh took his elbow off the shelf and straightened up. 'And to say welcome, of course. You're our newest staff member, after all.'

The new girl. Fresh meat...

'I do hope you're not hitting on me, Dr Stanmore.' Stevie dropped the plastic bag into the out tray for urgent lab tests and took a step back. 'I was just doing my job in helping you with that emergency and a simple "thank you" is more than enough.' There were more echoes in the back of her head and what she could feel roiling in her gut now was nothing like the pleasurable tickle of attraction.

'I'm your HOD. It's my duty to make my new staff members feel as welcome as possible. You're not going to say "no" to your boss on your first day at work, are you, Stephanie?'

Stevie swallowed hard but the internal

knot of something unpleasant, like anger, or possibly fear, was rapidly growing. She knew she shouldn't say anything more than offering a polite refusal of his invitation but, when she opened her mouth, something very different came out.

'Maybe in the old days it was generally accepted that a new nurse was fair game for every male in the vicinity.' Her tone was clipped. Controlled. Bordering on icy. 'I would hope we've all become a bit more enlightened these days when it comes to things like sexual harassment. Excuse *me*...' Stevie turned her back on her boss. 'I've got work to do.'

She didn't actually have to go into the supply room a little further down the corridor from the reception desk but it was the quickest way to escape the deathly silence behind her and the feeling of Josh Stanmore's gaze fixed on the back of her head as if it was the bullseye of a target. Stevie shoved open the door, let it swing shut behind her and then buried her face in her hands.

Oh... *God*... So much for her wonderful new start in life. She'd just ruined everything, hadn't she?

CHAPTER TWO

'I MEAN...WHAT'S her *problem*?' Josh tipped back the wooden chair he was sitting on so it was balancing on two legs. He tipped his head back as well, closing his eyes and letting his breath out in a long, weary sigh. 'I only offered to buy her a coffee, for heaven's sake, and she practically bit my head off. Even said something about sexual harassment, would you believe? I mean...*really*?'

'Hmm...' Nurse Manager Ruby's tone was noncommittal. She was still reading over what Josh had written in a section of her Critical Incident Report form. 'So your first attempt with the Magill's forceps failed?'

'Yes. It's remarkable how slippery a grape can be when it's coated with saliva. It was a delay in dealing with the obstructed airway of no more than twenty to thirty seconds and

there's no sign of any injury from oxygen de-
privation. She's a lucky kid.'

'She sure is,' Ruby agreed. 'We can be
very grateful that you spotted her. Who
knows how long it might have been before
someone had found her if you hadn't happened to walk past and look through that
window?'

'Oh…crazy new nurse would have found
her at almost the same time. She was carrying a bunch of toys back to the playroom.'
It was why he'd stopped, after all, because
he'd wanted the chance to talk to her. Not
that he would have done that if he'd had any
idea how prickly she was.

Ruby's glance, over her half-moon reading glasses, was exasperated. 'So now she's
crazy just because she didn't want to go on
a date with you?'

'It wasn't a *date*.'

'What was it, then?'

Josh resisted the urge to roll his eyes. 'It
was supposed to be a "thank you" for assisting me in an emergency. And a "welcome to
GG's paediatric ward".'

'Ah…' Ruby nodded sagely. 'And the fact
that she's young and gorgeous with that wild,
red hair and those big, brown eyes had noth-

ing to do with it? Tell me, Josh—if she was as old and ugly as me, would you have been so quick to offer to buy her a coffee?'

Josh grinned at Ruby. Okay, his most senior nurse was more than old enough to be his mother and she'd probably never had a particularly healthy BMI but she was not only one of the best nurses he'd ever worked with, she had a warmth that made it a real pleasure to be near her and a smile that could light up a room.

She was a wise old bird, too, and he had to admit there was some truth in what she was saying. He hadn't just been impressed with Stevie's professional skills this afternoon. At some level he'd also been perfectly well aware of exactly how attractive she was. He had *not* been hitting on her, however. He wouldn't think of doing that when he didn't even know if someone was single.

The errant thought that immediately followed—that he would quite *like* to know if Stevie was single—was easy to squash. His relationship with that new staff member was never going to be anything other than purely professional from now on. She hadn't quite slapped his face in public but it kind of felt like she had and he wasn't about to offer her an opportunity to repeat the put-down.

He let his chair thump back to the floor in time to see the mischievous tilt to Ruby's lips, which was enough to make him smile himself.

'I'll never understand women,' he admitted. 'Is that all you need from me for now, Ruby?'

Her face was deadpan now. 'Wouldn't mind a coffee,' she said. 'Milk and two sugars, thanks.'

'Ha...' As he stood up, the sleeve of his white coat knocked some papers from the corner of Ruby's desk. 'Sorry...' Josh bent to pick up the glossy pamphlets and, as he put them back on the desk, the picture on the front—a back view of a man and a boy walking in a park—caught his attention.

'What's this about?'

'Oh...' Ruby glanced up. 'Someone from the social services team left those with me today. It's about the Big Brother programme where men volunteer to be a kind of role model to young boys who don't have a father figure at home. Someone safe, like an uncle or a big brother—for tweens and teens, mostly, when they're more likely to go off the rails or be giving their family a hard time. We get quite a few solo mums through here and it's always good to be able to let them know what kind of community resources there are for getting support.'

She reached for a pen. 'I need to get you to sign this form before you rush off to get my coffee. Right there...'

He made two mugs of coffee in the staff-room and carried them back to Ruby's office a few minutes later. Her smile was a reward all by itself.

'You *did* get me a coffee. Always knew you were a good lad, Josh Stanmore.'

'You should have gone home a long time ago,' he told her. 'It's way past dinner time.'

'Oh, what's that?' Ruby tilted her head and looked up at the ceiling. 'Yeah...it's the pot calling the kettle black.' She closed her eyes as she took an appreciative sip of her hot drink.

'I'm going.' But Josh sat down on the wooden chair again. 'As soon as I've had this coffee, that is. I've been trying to get a chance to make it ever since that exciting little interruption we had this afternoon.'

Stevie would have gone home as least an hour ago, Josh thought. And then he gave himself a mental slap for even letting her enter his head. Needing distraction, he focused on the neat pile that those pamphlets were now in.

'Could have done with one of those,' he murmured.

'Oh?' Ruby was instantly alert. 'For a parent of one of our patients? You know something I don't know?'

'Doubt it. No... I was thinking of my own childhood. I got brought up by my grandmother. I could have done with someone like a big brother.' Not that he was about to tell Ruby, but he'd been one of those problem kids. He could have easily gone completely off the rails. 'Instead, I buried myself in my room and spent far too much time watching medical documentaries and crime shows. I was determined to be the world's best forensic pathologist.'

Ruby laughed. 'And you end up working with kids who never stop letting you know how alive they are by their screaming and kicking, filling their pants and throwing up on you? What went wrong there?'

Josh shrugged. 'They smile sometimes. And give you cuddles. Guess I just love kids. Maybe they make *us* feel more alive.'

Ruby's face softened. 'You're not wrong there. You should have some of your own one of these days.'

'Nah…' Josh drained his mug. 'Not going to happen. I've got more than enough of them here at work.'

He could feel Ruby's gaze following him as he left her office, though. He could almost hear her thinking that it was a shame he was going to miss out on so much by not wanting to have a family of his own but he wasn't about to tell anyone the reasons why he was never going to become a father.

The idea of being a 'big brother' was a new concept, however. How different would that be, to have a relationship with a child who wasn't sick? A child who might be living a life that was a very long way from being in one of those perfect, nuclear families? Or any kind of 'real' family?

He'd been that child once. And maybe that was at the core of the reasons he never wanted to try and create his own family but that was no excuse not to try and help another kid. It wasn't as if he didn't have plenty of spare time when he wasn't at work and he didn't even have a girlfriend making any demands on that spare time at the moment.

Charlotte from Radiology had crossed the line a few weeks ago when she'd given him the tearful ultimatum of either declaring his long-term commitment or admitting that their relationship was going nowhere. He'd been as kind as possible in making that admission but that particular scenario wasn't getting any easier to deal with due to familiarity. Why was it that women seemed to be so happy to sign up to a 'friendship with benefits' only to completely forget the clearly explained ground rules of a month or three later?

Oddly, he couldn't help wondering how Stevie would react to those ground rules and Josh found himself smiling wryly as he walked out of the front doors of Gloucester General Hospital. She wouldn't be reacting to any rules, would she? She'd be setting them all herself, like some sort of fierce headmistress in an exclusive school. Even more oddly, he had to admit that he admired that kind of ferocity enough for it to ramp up how attractive she was.

Josh shook his head, fishing in his pocket for his car keys. How immature was that? Hadn't he just been thinking he'd make a good role model as a big brother? This new nurse seemed to be creating unwanted ripples in his life—like a large stone being thrown into a pond he happened to be standing in for some inexplicable reason. He needed to get out of water, obviously.

And stay out…

'Stay here for the moment, please, Mrs Hawkesbury. Someone will be in to talk to you very soon.'

'It's Ms. I'm not married.'

'My apologies. It's not easy to—'

'I need to see my son.' Stevie interrupted the junior police officer who looked like he should still be in a school uniform rather than the one he was wearing. *'Please…'*

To her horror, she could hear the wobble in her voice and realised she was so wound up that it was quite possible she might burst into tears at any moment. Fifteen minutes ago, Ruby had taken one look at her face after the phone call she'd received and told her to leave work early without even asking for any explanation after hearing that it was a family problem.

'Go,' she'd told Stevie. *'I'll cover for you.'*

Her nurse manager was one in a million, that was for sure, but she'd already known that. When she'd confessed that she'd been rather rude to the head of their department, Ruby had actually chuckled.

'Don't you worry about that,' she'd said. *'He knows how well you do your job and it won't hurt him one little bit to get turned down for once.'*

'Matthew's fine.' The baby police officer gave her a reassuring smile. 'We don't make a habit of locking eleven-year-old boys up around here. He's actually having a game of snooker in our staffroom with one of our social workers, Tim. He'll bring him here as soon as you've had a chat with his boss, Angela. Ah…here she is. I'll leave you to it.'

Angela introduced herself as a liaison officer between the police and social services. '…and you're Stephanie, yes?'

'I prefer Stevie.'

Angela's smile was friendly. 'It's good to meet you, Stevie. Please, sit down.'

But Stevie remained standing. 'I need to know what's happening,' she said. 'I don't understand why he's been brought in here. He's a good kid. I know he'd *never* do something like shoplifting.'

'Please…'

The older woman's gesture towards the

seat was a command Stevie couldn't ignore and, to be honest, it was a bit of a relief to sit down. Her legs still hadn't recovered from how fast she'd run from the hospital to this police station. She was still wearing her scrubs under her coat.

'You're living on Hastings Street, yes?'

Stevie took a breath. She knew that high-density, inner-city living wasn't ideal for kids but it wasn't as if she was renting an apartment in some dodgy estate where she knew she'd be putting her son in danger.

'It's close to the hospital,' she defended herself. 'For my job. I'm a paediatric nurse. And there was a good school—King's—within walking distance for Mattie. We only moved here a few weeks ago.'

Angela's nod was sympathetic. 'The incident occurred at the corner shop on your street. Matthew was with a group of older boys and he was the only one the owner of the shop managed to catch. They were only stealing sweets but the owner's had trouble with this gang of lads for quite a while and he was fed up enough to call us in to try and give them a fright.'

A *gang*? Her serious, responsible boy was now part of a gang? Stevie shook her head.

'He was supposed to go straight home after school and get on with his homework. I'm paying one of the neighbours to keep an eye on him until I get home from work.'

'That would be Mrs Johnston?'

'That's right... How did you know?'

'We took Matthew home to start with and he told us about the arrangement but Mrs Johnston wasn't there. She'd left a note on the door to say she was sorry but that her daughter was sick and she'd had to go and collect her grandchildren. Anyway...that was why we decided to bring him back to the station for a while. Until we could contact you and have a chat.'

To see for themselves whether she was a responsible parent? Whether Social Services might need to be involved? Stevie could feel her hackles rising.

'I've been a single mother for more than eleven years,' she said. 'And we've managed just fine. We've never been in any kind of trouble with the police or anyone else. *Ever...*'

Oh, help... She needed to take a deep breath. 'I'm not saying it's been easy. Moving to Gloucester is a new start for us but... it's harder than I thought it would be, to settle in a new city. I know Mattie's finding it a bit difficult to get used to a new school. He's missing his old school friends.'

'Do you have any family nearby for support?'

Stevie shook her head. Her mother was hours away by train now. Twice as far as she'd been before she'd taken this huge step of starting a new life in this part of the country.

'Is Matthew's father involved?'

Stevie's head shake was a sharp dismissal of the idea. What would Angela think, she wondered, if she told her that the only involvement Mattie's father had ever had in his life had been to offer her enough money to get an abortion? She'd never told anyone that because she would never let her son know how unwanted he'd been by one of his parents. Despite how much the pregnancy had derailed the life she had planned for herself and how incredibly hard it had been at times, Mattie was the best thing that had ever happened for Stevie and she loved her little boy more than she'd known it was possible to love anyone.

Imagine if she'd been telling Angela about why he didn't have a father in his life when

Mattie was brought into the room by Tim the social worker—which was exactly what happened only moments after that question had been asked.

Stevie got to her feet, her arm outstretched to gather her son to her side, but Mattie had his head down and looked as though he was almost shrinking into himself—as if he was trying to hide? Stevie dropped her arm. He certainly didn't look as if he would welcome a hug from his mother right now.

Tim introduced himself and then turned to Angela. 'We've had a good chat, me and Matthew. I don't think he's going to be getting himself into any more trouble.' He smiled at Stevie. 'It's been a bit of a shock, coming here in the squad car.'

Stevie couldn't smile back. It had been more than a bit of a shock having had to run here, wondering if this was another blow to the dream of the new and wonderful life—like that unfortunate encounter with the chief consultant of her paediatric ward the other day. Surely history couldn't repeat itself to the extent that she'd need to pack up yet again and find another new start?

'We've had a talk about other things Matthew could be doing after school before you get home from work. Did you know that King's Primary School offers an after-school programme that runs until six o'clock?'

Stevie nodded. She also knew how expensive it was.

'I happen to know there are spaces held there for special kids.' Tim's tone was casual but the glance Stevie received over Mattie's head suggested that he'd read her mind. That these 'special' spaces were funded by some kind of charity?

Stevie could feel herself bristling again. She'd never accepted charity.

'You'd quite like to try it out, wouldn't you, Matthew? If I can sort it out for you?'

Mattie still wasn't making eye contact with his mother but he nodded in response to Tim's query.

'I'll be in touch, then. Here's my card, if you want to talk anytime. And there's something else I thought might possibly be of interest.' Tim handed Stevie a pamphlet. 'We won't hold you up any more now, though.' He patted Mattie's shoulder. 'It's been a pleasure meeting you,' he said. 'But I don't want to see you back here anytime soon, okay?'

Stevie barely glanced at the pamphlet but she could see it had a picture of a man and

a boy walking in some idyllic-looking park.
She shoved it into her shoulder bag.

'Let's go, Mattie. It's time we went home.'

Her legs still felt strangely heavy as she
got to her feet, however. Her heart was feeling a bit on the heavy side, as well. It didn't
really feel like they were heading home at
all, especially with how Mattie still had his
head down as he was walking, scuffing his
feet and refusing to respond to Stevie's at-
tempts to talk to him with anything more
than grunts.

'I'm not cross,' she told him. 'I'm guessing
you only did what you did because you were
trying to fit in. Or make friends...?'

Her suggestion earned a shrug, along with
a sound that was equally noncommittal.

'We'll talk about it later, okay? After dinner. Don't know about you, but I'm absolutely starving.'

The elevator in their apartment block was
out of order. Again. Stevie had already been
on her feet for so long it was a real effort to
climb flight after flight of stairs. At least she
didn't have to worry about hauling a pram
with her these days but she'd been wrong to
think that life would magically get so much
easier as Mattie got older. The challenges

of being a single parent to a tiny baby had been enormous but, in retrospect, they had been simple.

Mattie was now old enough and responsible enough to be able to keep himself clean and fed and entertained but the challenges were still there and seemed to be becoming far more complex.

At some point, preferably later this evening, they were going to have to talk about all this and she could only hope they could work together to find a new approach that might help. If she had to swallow her pride and accept assistance that could give her boy access to resources like an after-school programme that might provide both company and enjoyment then so be it.

At least she had Mattie's favourite food in the freezer and it wasn't bad parenting to allow a meal like fish fingers, chips and maybe a fried egg for a treat, was it—even if there wasn't going to be a green vegetable in sight?

This wasn't going well.

The lad had barely said anything during their introductory meeting so far.

'This was my mum's idea, not mine.' He

got up from his chair and went to stare out the window. The room in this downtown building looked out over a busy road. 'I don't need a big brother.'

'She's coming today as well, yes?' Josh looked over the boy's head to where the social worker, Tim, was sitting on the other side of the room.

Tim nodded. 'She texted to say she's running a bit late, but if Mattie was happy, we could go ahead and make a plan for what you're going to do next time.'

Josh was starting to wonder if there was going to be a next time. This serious young boy didn't look as if he was going to welcome a stranger into his life. Only eleven years old and he was clearly practised in protecting himself. How sad was that? Sad enough to remind Josh of things about his own childhood that he'd buried long ago, anyway. He got up, moving to stand beside the lad at the window. He didn't say anything—he just wanted to let him get used to him being close—but it seemed to have an instant effect of making the boy freeze.

It was the gasp of horror that made Josh realise that Mattie wasn't even aware of him standing there, however, and a split second later, the screech of brakes and then a squeal of tyres alerted him to what Mattie had been witnessing. A small dog had been hit by a car that was now accelerating away into heavy traffic, leaving the animal on the side of the road.

'*No...*' Mattie's face was white, which made his eyes look even darker and more horrified as he looked up at Josh. He was trying hard not to cry. 'It's...dead, isn't it?'

'No.' Josh glanced back through the window. 'Look...he's trying to get up now. Looks like he's hurt his leg, though. Shall we go and see if we can help?'

Mattie's nod was vehement and he caught his breath, poised to bolt towards the door. Josh caught Tim's gaze to check that it was okay to go outside with Mattie, seeing as they were only supposed to be having a family meeting here at the organisation's headquarters today. Tim was nodding.

'Josh is a doctor, Mattie. I'm sure he'll be able to help that dog.'

There wasn't much they could do on the street, mind you, and there was nobody who seemed to be with the dog so Josh carried it back into the building. Tim found some towels and other things that Josh requested and Mattie crouched on the floor, staring intently at what Josh was doing as he examined the small, scruffy terrier.

'I don't think he's badly hurt,' Josh told him. 'But, can you see that?'

'What?'

'The shape of his leg?'

'It's different to the other leg, isn't it?'

'Well spotted.' Josh smiled at Mattie. 'And smart. That's one of the things they teach us to do at medical school when we're trying to find out what's wrong—to compare one side with the other to see if it's different. What do you reckon the problem is?'

'Is it broken?'

'I think so.' Josh's touch was very gentle but the dog yelped in pain.

Mattie reached out to stroke the wiry little head.

'Be careful. Even a friendly dog can bite if it's in pain or really scared.'

'He's not going to bite,' Mattie said. The dog whimpered but he had closed his eyes at the touch, as if it was comforting him.

'He hasn't got a collar,' Tim said. 'And he's pretty dirty. I reckon he's a stray, which could mean that nobody's going to want to pay a big vet's bill.'

'I'll pay it,' Josh said. 'Is there a vet near here that you know of?'

'I'll look it up.' Tim picked up his phone.

'We'll need to make this little guy a bit more comfortable to take him to the vet,' Josh told Mattie. 'What I'll do is wrap a towel around his leg and then you can help me bandage it into a kind of splint.'

'There's a vet clinic just a couple of blocks away,' Tim reported a minute or two later.

'Right. I'll take him there now.' Josh used another towel to wrap and scoop up the dog.

'I'm coming too,' Mattie said. He was already beside the door, his face both anxious but determined.

Tim hesitated. Josh could see he knew he shouldn't be breaking the Big Brother protocol of a supervised first meeting but this was an emergency. It had also been enough to break through the obvious reluctance Mattie had had to connect with somebody new. If he was forced to stay behind, he might well retreat behind barriers that would be even harder to breach.

'Okay,' Tim said, finally. 'But you stay with Josh, Mattie. And don't leave the clinic.

I'll bring your mum down as soon as she arrives.'

Mattie's gaze was fixed on the face of the little dog that was all that could be seen amongst the folds of the towel but then he glanced up at Josh and the expression on the boy's face just melted his heart. He would never let it show, in front of relatives or even his colleagues, but there were times Josh felt that desperate to help a vulnerable baby or small child who was critically ill. Because of that, he knew how important it was to feel as if you could make a difference.

'This little guy's not too heavy,' he said quietly to Mattie. 'And I know he trusts you. Do you think you could carry him?'

He could almost see the inches of height Mattie gained as he straightened up and nodded solemnly. As Josh placed the injured dog carefully into the boy's arms, he caught his gaze again and that squeeze on his heart was there even more than before. This scruffy little dog had done more than provide a way for him to connect with this lad. By trusting Mattie to help with his care, Josh had taken a big step towards winning the trust of a child who reminded him of his much younger self.

And it felt like the best thing that had happened to Josh in longer than he could remember.

'Come on…' He held the door open for Mattie. 'Let's do this…'

It was the second time in little more than a week that Stevie had had the stress of racing through the inner-city streets of Gloucester with no idea of exactly what she was heading towards.

At least it wasn't a police station this time but the fact that it involved someone from Social Services was enough to generate anxiety—especially given that Stevie was now very late for the appointment to meet the mentor Mattie had been paired with at the Big Brother programme. She was hardly going to come across as a shining example of great parenting when she couldn't even turn up on time and Stevie also had a horrible feeling that, even though she'd showered and completely changed her clothes, she might still be carrying the taint of the unpleasant incident of the vomiting child that had delayed her departure from work.

Even more worryingly, Tim the social worker was standing on the wide front step of the address she'd been given, clearly watching out for her.

'Has something happened? Where's Mattie?'

Oh, help…had he run away or something? He hadn't been that keen on the idea of coming here in the first place but, after that long talk they'd had about different things they could do to help him settle in a new home, he'd agreed to give it a go.

'He's just down the road, with his mentor, Josh. It's okay…' Tim added hurriedly as he saw Stevie's expression. 'I'll explain on the way to the vet clinic. I just wanted to tell you face to face rather than with a text message that might have worried you.'

By the time they arrived at the vet clinic, Stevie had been given the impression that the dog's accident might have been a good thing and provided a much faster route than normal for a relationship to develop between a boy who might be in need of a male role model and his mentor.

It was a bit of a shame that the match had been made with someone that had the same name as the man she was now doing her best to avoid in her new job but she could get past that if it was going to be a good thing for

Mattie. Any interaction with Dr Stanmore had been minimal since she'd been so rude to him and she hadn't even seen him in the distance today so it was easy to dismiss anything negative that the name stirred up.

Besides, she was focused on Mattie as they were shown into the consulting room at the clinic. She hadn't seen him look like this in a very long time—as if it was Christmas morning when he'd still been young enough to believe in the magic of Santa Claus, with the way his whole face was shining with excitement.

'Mum…look… I helped fix his broken leg. He's had X-rays and everything and I helped make the plaster cast. And Josh let me carry him all the way here and…he doesn't have a chip so Josh says maybe he doesn't even have a family and…can we take him home? Please…?'

Oh, my… Stevie opened her mouth and then closed it again. What on earth could she say? As soon as Mattie was told that there were strict rules in their apartment building that no pets were allowed, she was going to see that animation—joy, even—drain from his face. She glanced at Tim but he just gave her a sympathetic look. The vet could see she needed help, however.

'We can keep him overnight,' she said. 'There are some animal rescue sites on social media that we can put his photo on and, who knows, maybe we'll find he does have an owner so he won't need to go to the pound.'

'No...'

Mattie shook his head, turning away to look up at the man standing just behind him. A moment of silent communication that covered the shock of Stevie discovering that the name of the mentor her son had been paired with was not just a coincidence. That he was none other than the most senior doctor in her department and the man she'd practically accused of sexually harassing her.

'I'll take him,' Josh Stanmore said. 'While we're looking for his owner, anyway.'

'Can I come and visit him, then?' Mattie's tone was a plea. 'Next time I see you?'

Next time? Oh, no... Stevie felt like the walls were starting to close in on her. Mattie wanted to see Josh again? Wanted to have a relationship with her boss? Surely Josh wouldn't be comfortable with that any more than she was?

But he was smiling at Mattie. 'I think

that's up to your mum,' he said. 'That was the deal, remember? We were all going to meet today and talk about what happens next.'

Mattie nodded, turning back to fix his gaze on his mother.

'But you *said*, Mum…' His tone was accusing now. 'You told Tim that if I was happy we could plan what was going to happen next time.'

Across the top of his head, Josh was also staring at Stevie and it felt almost like the two of them were ganging up on her.

What was Josh even doing here? Surely he had enough to do with children in his working life? He might have a few at home as well as far as she knew but, in any case, a Big Brother match was inappropriate given her professional relationship with this man. It could also be extremely awkward. Imagine what Mattie might tell Josh about her? It already felt as if her privacy had been severely breached here.

It couldn't possibly be allowed to happen, that was all there was to it, but this was going to have to be handled carefully. Things were fragile enough with Mattie to make disappointing him a big deal. This could turn out to be a turning point and Stevie needed time to think because the last thing she wanted was to make things worse. She knew her words were the classic parental cop-out but it was the best she could come up with under this kind of pressure.

'I'll have to think about it,' she said. 'We'll see.'

CHAPTER THREE

IT HAD TO HAPPEN, of course.

There was no way Josh could avoid seeing Stevie at work and, to be honest, he didn't want to avoid it. He'd been sharing his home for a couple of days now with a small, scruffy dog who had a plaster cast on its leg so it couldn't move very much, and Josh couldn't catch sight of the injured animal or carry it out to the garden for bathroom business without thinking of the boy who'd helped him rescue it.

A boy who reminded him of things that had shaped his own life. Like the loneliness. Like feeling that he didn't belong, or worse, that he wasn't wanted. That need to help others in order to make himself feel worthwhile. Good grief... Mattie even looked a bit like Josh had at that age, being a bit tall and lean for his age, with shaggy dark hair and brown eyes.

He wanted to know that Mattie was okay after the trauma of seeing that accident. He wanted to let him know that the dog was doing great and the only way he could do that was to speak to Mattie's mother.

He just hadn't expected that it would come in the wake of more drama. Or that it would be Stevie who slipped into the treatment room as he stood there, unable to get on with the procedure he was there to perform. Unable to move, in fact, seeing as he was scrubbed and keeping his gloved hands from touching anything non-sterile. Fortunately, his small patient was sedated enough to be asleep on the bed in front of him and it was also fortunate that Stevie was clearly up to speed with what was going on. She had already pulled a gown over her scrubs and was reaching for a mask from the wall dispenser.

'Ruby said you need a hand for a lumbar puncture.'

'Mmm… This is Taylor. Her mum needed to step outside for a minute, along with Ruby and my registrar.'

'Yes.' Stevie didn't meet his eyes as she went to the other side of the bed. 'I found her inhaler but your registrar decided they needed to get her down to ED.'

'It was a rather dramatic onset of an asthma attack. She was a bit overwhelmed by all this.'

Stevie simply nodded, as if she knew exactly why Taylor's mother had been so upset. She bent down so that her face was close to that of the five-year-old girl. 'Hey, sweetheart,' she said softly. 'My name's Stevie.'

Oh…man… That note in Stevie's voice when she'd said 'sweetheart'. It was as though it had struck some weird kind of gong buried deep in Josh's chest. He could feel a reverberation of the single word that was giving him the strangest feeling of…what was it… *longing*? Or maybe it was sadness that he'd never heard anyone call *him* 'sweetheart' like that. As if they were so completely and utterly genuine.

Maybe that note had been what had pierced Taylor's sleepiness, although her words were slurred enough to suggest a good level of sedation as her eyes fluttered open. 'Where's Mummy?'

'She'll be back soon. She asked me to help look after you.' Stevie stroked wisps of blonde hair back from Taylor's face. 'I'm going to help you stay really, really still for Dr Josh, okay?'

''kay...'

'I can see you've got someone to cuddle. Is it a rabbit?''

'Is Bunny...' The girl's arms tightened around the stuffed toy she was clutching.

'You cuddle Bunny...' Stevie's murmur was reassuring. 'And I'm going to cuddle you...'

Taylor's eyes drifted shut again as Stevie moved her hands to a position where she could make sure the child couldn't move suddenly. She looked up at Josh.

'You happy with her position? Do you want the spine flexed any more than this?'

For a heartbeat, Josh was caught by Stevie's eyes. Mesmerised, even. Perhaps it was because her face was half-covered by a mask so it was her eyes that were more obvious. Or maybe it was because he hadn't noticed before that those eyes were such an extraordinary colour. A tawny kind of hazel with the same golden glints that were shining amongst the red in that wild hair of hers under the bright light above this table. As alive as the flicker of flames.

The moment was no more than a blink

of time. 'Position's good,' Josh said crisply. 'We're all set up with the skin preparation, sterile drapes and the tubes ready. Topical anaesthesia should be completely effective by now but I wasn't going to start subcutaneous anaesthesia without being sure she wasn't going to move.'

'Of course.'

Josh could see the way Stevie spread her fingers and increased the pressure where she was holding Taylor's shoulders and hips to maintain vertical alignment of the spine. It wasn't the first time that he'd realised she knew exactly what she was doing and it gave him absolute confidence to continue with this delicate procedure.

He drew an imaginary line between the iliac crests, knowing that where the line intersected with the spine would be approximately the space between the L3 and L4 discs. His small patient didn't seem to be aware of the fine needle he used to slowly infiltrate the area with local anaesthetic. It was such an automatic skill that Josh realised he was still a little too aware of who it was that was assisting him and he needed to remind himself that this was nothing other than a professional interaction.

'Taylor came in with a fever, headache and unusual drowsiness. She said her legs ached and she has a bit of a rash on one leg.'

'Oh…' Stevie's subtle nod was an understanding of why it was a priority to take a sample of cerebral spinal fluid to find out whether the symptoms were being caused by something as serious as meningitis. Then she tilted her head so that she could see Taylor's face while still holding her in position. 'That's no good, is it, sweetheart? Not nice having sore legs.' She glanced back at Josh. 'Sound asleep,' she whispered.

Josh nodded. He was completely focused now as he reached for the lumbar puncture needle, holding it with the bevel pointing to the ceiling before carefully piercing the skin and then pausing to wait for any movement from his patient. Stevie had her head very close to Taylor's face. Josh couldn't hear what she was murmuring but it was obviously enough to distract the little girl from what he was doing because she barely even twitched. He advanced the needle, feeling the increased resistance of the spinous ligament and then further until he felt that resistance fade. He removed the stylet from inside the needle and was relieved to see the drops of fluid appear. He only needed to collect five to ten drops in the two sterile tubes so this would all be over very soon, having created minimal distress for his newest patient.

'Speaking of sore legs,' he said quietly, as he held the first tube in place to catch the drops, 'come and find me when you've got a spare moment later. I've got something to show you.'

He was making it look so easy but Stevie knew how much skill that took. Josh's confidence probably had a lot to do with the calm atmosphere in this treatment room as well. It was nothing like the tension they had worked under the first time they'd been in there together. This was so gentle that Taylor wasn't even waking up. So gentle that Stevie felt like it was a privilege to be this close to him and working alongside him like this.

Maybe she'd been stressing far too much in the last couple of days about how awkward it was going to be if—or more likely when— she had to interact with her HOD again. She hadn't detected anything negative in his expression when he'd seen who had been sent to assist him. If anything, Josh almost looked as if he was pleased to see her again after her days off. Which was why, when she saw him a couple of hours later, in the early afternoon, it felt easy to offer him a smile.

'Spare moment alert,' she said. 'It's my lunch break.' She held up a paper bag as proof.

Josh smiled back. A quick, easy grin that made his face light up, in fact. A smile that gave Stevie a curious burst of something… warmth, perhaps…that popped and spread somewhere deep inside her gut. Dark eyes always looked warm but there was something about the way Josh's eyes crinkled at the corners and one slightly out of line tooth provided the charm of an imperfection that took that smile to the next level.

'Perfect timing,' he told her. 'Follow me.'

He headed towards the smoke-stop door by the elevators that led to the stairwell. Oddly, it didn't occur to Stevie to hesitate in following him, even when he took the stairs two at a time to go past the highest level of this hospital block and onto the roof space. Built in a U shape, this wing of Gloucester General Hospital was directly opposite the one with the helipad and fast access to the emergency department on the ground floor. She'd never been up here before, of course, but what was surprising was that she hadn't heard about this space.

'It's a…a *vegetable* garden?' Stevie couldn't count the number of raised beds that were awash with greenery. There were even fruit trees in huge planter boxes. People were working on the other side of the roof and seemed to be filling a container with freshly dug carrots.

'Isn't it great? The idea got started by some volunteers a few years back and it's kept growing…so to speak.' Josh was grinning again. 'I love coming up here for a few minutes when I get a break. There are seats—see? And a great view. If there wasn't so much forest or so many hills out there, I'd be able to see the village I live in.'

'That's why I wanted to come here,' Stevie said. 'My dream was to get out of a big city and live in one of those Cotswold villages. Inner-city Gloucester isn't ideal but at least we're out of London now. One step closer…'

Josh's sideways glance was curious but he didn't say anything other than to suggest a bench to sit on.

'Go ahead and have your lunch,' he added, after they'd both sat down. 'I know how precious any time to eat is around here.'

'Have you eaten already?'

Josh shook his head. 'It can wait.'

'Have one of these.' Stevie offered him the bag. 'Mousetraps are Mattie's favourite lunch but I made far too many of them yesterday.'

Josh took one of the baked triangles of toast and cheese and bit into it. Seconds later, his face lit up again. 'I'm with Mattie,' he said. 'These are *so* good.'

'Dead easy.' Stevie shrugged off the compliment. Because she was actually trying to shrug off an even stronger dose of that warmth his smile had created earlier. 'It's just a bit of Vegemite on toast and then grated cheese and egg on top and you bake them in the oven until they're crispy. Have another one.' She held the bag out again but avoided meeting Josh's gaze. Instead, she looked around at the planter boxes. 'And thanks for showing me this. It's amazing.'

'Oh…' Josh paused as he reached towards the bag and then put his hand in his pocket instead. 'That's not what I wanted to show you. Here…' He had his phone in his hand now and he tapped the screen to reveal a photograph. 'I gave him a bath last night— as best I could while keeping the cast dry with a plastic bag, anyway. He looks like a different dog, doesn't he?'

Stevie looked at a much whiter, fluffier version of the little stray terrier she'd seen at the vet clinic. 'He certainly looks a lot happier.'

'He's loving my garden. I have someone from the village who helps me with housework and stuff and she's keeping an eye on Lucky during the day.'

'Lucky?'

'It was Mattie's idea for a name. Because he'd been lucky not to have been killed when that car hit him.' Josh hesitated for a moment. 'I thought he might like to see this picture. If you give me your number, I'll send it to you.' He tapped his screen again to open his contacts.

Silently Stevie took the phone and began to input her details. 'He'll love that,' she said quietly. 'He's been desperate for some news. Not that he's saying much.'

'How come?'

'He doesn't want to talk to me.' Stevie handed back the phone. 'He thinks I'm going to say he can't see you—or Lucky—again.'

'And are you?' Josh was holding her gaze.

'Well…it's not really appropriate, is it?'

'Why not?'

'We work together. And…' Stevie bit her

lip but the genuine concern in Josh's expression overcame her hesitation. 'And I don't understand why you want to be doing it in the first place. You're a bit old to be a Big Brother, aren't you?'

'Fair call.' Josh nodded. 'I'm thirty-six,' he admitted. 'And that's the upper limit for being involved as a mentor but I'd never heard of the organisation until I saw a brochure that Ruby had. The more I thought about it, the more I liked the idea. Meeting Mattie only made me even more sure. He's such a great kid, Stevie. You can be very proud of what you've achieved as a parent.'

The praise was so heartfelt it almost brought the prickle of tears to Stevie's eyes.

'You should have seen how gentle he was with Lucky,' Josh continued quietly. 'He was quite prepared to risk getting bitten so he could look after him and so fierce in his determination to make sure that little dog was going to be okay.' The corner of his mouth curled upwards. 'Bit like his mum was when she was helping me deal with a totally obstructed airway once.'

Stevie ducked her head. More praise? It felt like Josh genuinely liked her. Admired her, even?

'I grew up without a dad,' Josh added softly. 'Without much of a family, in fact. I got adopted but then they changed their minds down the track. I reckon I could have done with a "Big Brother" back then. Mattie told me that his dad died before he was born. That he just had you and his gran.'

Stevie bit her lip. That Josh had been adopted and then given up was such a personal thing to be sharing with someone who was pretty much a stranger and she could see way beneath those matter-of-fact words. She could see a small boy—who might actually look a bit like her Mattie, come to think of it—who was feeling lonely and unwanted. All she wanted to do was to reach back in time and hug that boy. To tell him that it was going to be okay. That he was going to grow up to be a rather extraordinary man, in fact.

Instead, she closed her eyes and let her breath out in a sigh because the most personal thing she'd carried around as a secret for so many years was suddenly overwhelming her. Why on earth it felt like Josh Stanmore was someone she could trust as the first person to share it with was too extraordinary to try and analyse but it probably had a lot to do with what he'd just told her about his childhood. Anyway, it was there and she felt…safe.

'Mattie's father didn't die before he was born,' she whispered. 'He just didn't want either of us. He did die in a car accident a few years later but, at the time, he just gave me more than enough money to get an abortion and find a job in another hospital—preferably as far away as I could get. It was only then that I found out he already had a wife. And kids. I don't ever want Mattie to know how unwanted he was by his dad. It was easier to pretend he was already dead and just get on with being the best parent I could be all by myself.'

Josh was silent for so long that Stevie cringed. Her father, who'd also died a couple of years ago, had thought his daughter was ruining her life by the choices she was making at the time. That she was compounding her carelessness by stupidity. And even though she'd got past a lot of negative judgement from people over the years, she really didn't want more of the same from Josh.

She didn't get it. Instead, he caught her gaze and his face was very still and serious.

'So…you're brave as well as beautiful,'

he said. 'But I think I already guessed that much.'

He thought she was beautiful? Oh…*my*… There was a flood of warmth deep inside her that clearly had nothing to do with the way this man smiled.

'And you make the best mousetraps ever,' Josh added, as if he was trying to lighten the atmosphere. Or give her an escape if she needed one? 'I'd better get back to work.'

As if to speed him along, his pager beeped. Josh read the message and Stevie heard the relief in the way he released his breath.

'Taylor's results from the lumbar puncture are back. She hasn't got meningitis.'

'Oh, thank goodness for that. Her mum will be so relieved.'

'She will—so I'd better scoot so I can pass on the good news.' Josh stood up but he was eyeing Stevie's paper bag. 'I don't suppose I could take another one of those with me?'

Stevie grinned. 'Help yourself.'

Josh turned away, a triangle of toast in his hand, but Stevie found herself frowning. She was puzzled.

'Why did you bring me all the way up here to show me a photo?' she asked. 'You could have done that in the staffroom.'

Josh looked over his shoulder. 'I got the feeling that you're like me. That you wouldn't like having your private life gossiped about. Any secrets are safe with me, Stevie.'

The thought came instantly. Mattie would be safe with him, too. And nobody here would have to know anything about it, would they?

Stevie could feel a smile taking over her lips. 'I don't think I've shared a real secret since I had my first best friend at primary school.'

'I've never told anyone mine,' Josh said around a mouthful of mousetrap. 'I guess that means we're friends?'

Stevie had to laugh. 'I guess it does.'

Her smile faded as she watched him walk towards the stairwell door. Had he really chosen her as the first person to share an intimate secret with? She'd already known that Josh Stanmore was a brilliant doctor and totally dedicated to his young patients but she was aware of far deeper layers to this man now. He'd had a tough upbringing but he had reached a level of education and skill that made him a leader in his field. He'd seen her son's best qualities within a short time of being with him and he was caring enough to want to follow up on that meeting, which made him perceptive and kind and… and possibly the most genuinely nice person that Stevie had ever met.

Mattie deserved to have someone like Josh in his life as a role model, she decided. And if she felt like it might be awkward because she worked with Josh, then maybe she just needed to get over herself.

It could work. At least she was quite sure of one thing she had learned about Josh Stanmore today.

She could trust him, which meant she was as safe with him as Mattie would be.

No. Make that two things. As impossible as it seemed, it really felt like Josh could see her for who she really was. That he not only understood what made her tick but that he approved of her.

Liked her…?

So, yeah… As unexpected as it was, it did seem like they were already friends. She sat amongst the vegetable gardens for a few more minutes, to eat the rest of her lunch, but when she got up to go back to work, Stevie found she was still a little puzzled. Josh had said he had someone to help him with his housework. Did that mean he lived alone?

Surely not... The man was gorgeous. He was also talented, confident, successful and had the ability to make a woman feel more than a little special. For the vast majority of women, that would be a totally irresistible combination.

Thank goodness she wasn't in that majority. That she was pretty much immune, even to charm and charisma on that kind of level.

'So...what can you see, Mattie?'

'You can still see where it was broken.'

'But can you see that new bone growth around the break?' Josh touched the smudged area on the illuminated X-ray in the vet's consulting room. 'Do you remember what that's called?'

'A...fracture...um...callus?'

'Wow...' Jill, the vet, sounded impressed. 'Have you been studying orthopaedics, Mattie?'

'Josh is teaching me.' Mattie seemed to grow an inch as he straightened. 'He's my Big Brother.' His face brightened. 'Did you know that the bones of dogs and cats are almost exactly the same as the arms and legs of people?'

It was Josh's turn to be impressed because

there was no hint of amusement on Jill's face at being given a basic animal anatomy tip.

'I did know that,' she said. 'It's fascinating, isn't it? Do you know the name of the bone that Lucky broke?'

'He broke two,' Mattie said confidently. 'The tibia and…' He looked up at Josh. 'And the fibia?'

'Fibula,' he supplied.

'Oh, yeah… I remember now. And it was an oblique fracture.'

This time Jill did laugh. 'I think someone's after my job. What's the treatment plan now, Mattie?'

But Mattie shrugged, suddenly shy, and Josh was reminded of the first official sessions he'd had with Stevie's son after getting the surprising news that she had agreed that he could become Mattie's mentor. It was a good thing that nobody had come looking for Lucky yet because that was the connection Josh had been able to build on as they took the small dog for outings in the park, taking turns to carry him.

The dog wouldn't be ready to chase a ball anytime soon, either.

'I'm very happy with the way the bone is healing,' Jill told them, 'but Lucky needs to keep the cast on for another few weeks yet. He might have a bit of a limp for a while after that, too.' She glanced at Josh. 'You still planning to keep him?'

He could feel the sudden tension in the room as Mattie's body went very still.

'For now,' he said. 'There's obviously no one trying to find him and I've got used to having him around. I really like the little guy.'

Mattie said nothing more until they were out of the clinic and had tucked Lucky back into his crate in the back of Josh's Jeep. For the first time, he wasn't going to take Mattie back to Big Brother Headquarters to wait for Stevie to collect him. He was going to drop Mattie back home himself.

But Mattie wasn't looking too pleased about the new arrangement. He was scowling as he responded to Josh's reminder to put his seat belt on.

'What's up?'

'How long is "for now"?' Mattie demanded.

'Sorry, what?' Josh started the engine.

'You said you were only going to keep Lucky "for now". That means you're going to give him away later, doesn't it?'

Josh killed the engine. The depth of emotion in this lad's dark eyes wrapped itself straight around his heart like a vice.

'There's only one person I'd ever give Lucky to,' he told Mattie. 'And that's you, buddy. As long as no one turns up to claim him, he's kind of *our* dog, isn't he?'

The way Mattie struggled to swallow made it obvious how close to tears he'd been. He turned away to stare out the side window. 'We're not allowed dogs in our apartment,' he muttered.

'I know.' Josh started up the car again. 'But your mum told me that, one day, she wanted to live in one of the villages around here.'

Mattie was silent again, until they got close to his address. 'Can I really have Lucky, if Mum and I get to live in a proper house?'

'We'd have to talk to your mum about that but, if she said yes and nobody else has said that Lucky belongs to them, then I'd be more than happy for you to have Lucky. I know how well you'd look after him.'

Mattie thought about that as Josh parked the car. 'Mum said it's really expensive to get a house but, after she's been in her new job for a while, she's going to go and talk to the bank about getting a mortgage.'

'Hmm...' Josh needed to shut down this line of conversation. 'That sounds like a good plan.'

Stevie's financial situation was none of Josh's business, even if they were friends. And they *were* friends. They'd shared secrets, hadn't they? And mousetraps. The unfortunate misunderstanding of that first meeting was forgiven and forgotten. They had an easy, enjoyable professional relationship and a connection that nobody else at Gloucester General knew anything about and Josh wasn't about to break the trust that had been put in him as Mattie's mentor.

Mattie was learning to trust him, too and the most surprising thing about that was how important it felt to Josh. Life changing, even. He was being gifted a position of huge influence in the life of a young boy—maybe even the kind of relationship he might have had as a father if he'd chosen to take that path in life.

He was never going to have a son of his own. There were too many children in the world who weren't getting the best of what life—and families—could offer. They were missing out. Like he had. Like Mattie was, even though he had the most amazing mother. What Josh hadn't expected was to feel like winning Mattie's trust was the best thing that had ever happened to him.

That he would do whatever it took not to let anything break a trust like that.

Not ever.

Oh, *help*…

She'd only expected Josh to drop Mattie off in front of the apartment block, not come up four flights of stairs with him. Should she ask him to come in? Offer him a coffee or something?

Stevie could feel the curse of the red-head sneaking up on her as spots of warmth bloomed on her cheeks. This was awkward, which was a shame because it had become so easy to be around Josh at work in the last few weeks. Maybe it was awkward because it reminded her of the way she'd slapped him down so harshly when he'd offered *her* coffee…

And then it was suddenly, blindingly obvious.

He hadn't been hitting on her that day, at all. He'd just been being friendly. Welcoming. The way she felt she ought to be right now.

Mattie was pushing past her to get into

the apartment. 'We took Lucky to the vet,' he told her. 'And it was so cool. I got to help with the X-ray. I had to wear this really heavy apron thing. Can I call Gran and tell her all about it?'

'Yes,' Stevie called after him. 'But hang your coat up first and don't leave your school-bag there...' She turned to smile at Josh. 'Would you like a coffee or something?'

The beat of hesitation, and the flash of something she couldn't quite interpret in his eyes, told Stevie that Josh was also remembering that unfortunate first encounter at work. But...maybe that was amusement she could see in his face? A dismissal of something that would never have been an issue if they'd known what they knew now about each other.

And, weirdly, Stevie was aware of something that was almost disappointment. As if she'd prefer that he had been hitting on her and that, now that they knew each other better, he might think of doing it again...

Wow...maybe she wasn't quite as immune to this man's charisma as she'd thought she was.

Not that it would make any difference. Her initial worry that it would be inappropriate to be working with the man who had become a 'Big Brother' to her son had proved unfounded. What would, however, be completely unacceptable was anything *more* than a professional relationship or a friendship between them.

For a very intense moment, Stevie could imagine that she could see her own thoughts being mirrored in Josh's eyes and it felt as if the attraction was mutual. Almost in the same instant, however, Josh broke that eye contact and the moment evaporated.

'Tell Mattie I'll think up somewhere more interesting than the park for us to go to next week. And I'll see you at work, Stevie.'

It was definitely a relief to close the front door of her apartment and, for a long moment, Stevie stayed where she was. She didn't need to remind herself that this was all about Mattie. Or that she'd never hesitated to make sacrifices in her life that were necessary to put her precious child first. What was one more?

It wasn't as if she needed a man in her life because she was obviously coping perfectly well without one. And it wasn't as if Josh was feeling the same attraction. It was unfortunate that an almost forgotten part of her life—and her body—had chosen to wake up right now but it wasn't anything she couldn't handle. Lifting her chin, she turned away from the door. Towards her family.

'Is Gran still on the line, Mattie?' she called. 'I'd like to talk to her too.'

CHAPTER FOUR

IT HAD BECOME something of a ritual, picking up the glossy real estate magazine from outside a nearby agency when she and Mattie went out to get groceries on a Thursday evening. After dinner and any chores were completed, they would both have an hour or so to treat themselves. Mattie would play his computer games. Stevie would find a picture-perfect Cotswold cottage for sale and clip the advertisement from the magazine to add to her collection. It was still a dream but it was starting to feel as if it wasn't a stupid dream because life was getting steadily better as she and Mattie settled into their new lives.

There were still things to worry about, of course—like the gang of local boys who'd persuaded Mattie to shoplift and got him into trouble with the police. He was managing to stay away from them but that was apparently causing problems. Not that Mattie was saying anything, but Stevie suspected he was getting bullied on a regular basis because of something Josh had told her today. That was another ritual that was adding pleasure to her life—meeting Josh amongst the vegetable gardens on the roof on the odd occasions their lunch breaks coincided.

'It was just a bit of name-calling going on from down the street when I walked home with him.'

'Like what?'

'He asked me to promise not to tell you. He's very protective of you, Stevie.'

'So you're not going to tell me?'

'Can't break a promise.'

But there had been reassurance in that gaze. If it was something that could compromise Mattie's safety, she could be sure that Josh would tell her anything she needed to know.

'Is there anything else I should know about?'

'Well...he misses his mates from his old school.'

'Yeah... I know that.'

'And he misses his grandma.'

'I know that too. I was going to get Mum to

*come and visit us but there's just not enough
room in our apartment. Or hers, either. She
moved into a tiny unit in a retirement village
last year and there's only a two-seater couch
as an extra bed.'*

She'd hoped she wouldn't need to spell out
that other accommodation was beyond her
budget.

*'He reckons he's old enough to go by him-
self. On the train.'*

Stevie had shaken her head.

*'He's too young to go that far by himself.
What if he got off at the wrong station?'*

*'A bus, then? The driver could keep an eye
on him. And maybe your mum could meet
him at the other end.'*

Stevie could almost hear the sound of
Josh's voice as she remembered their conversation and she let her head rest on the back of
her chair as she closed her eyes and let that
awareness wash over her. Had he and Mattie already discussed this and come up with
a plan during one of their weekly sessions?
A flash of something that could have been
jealousy rippled through Stevie at the thought
of Mattie confiding in someone other than
herself but, in virtually the same instant, she
was both touched that Mattie was trying to

protect her from worry about him and aware that she had to give Josh credit for being a big part of why their lives were so much better. Both her own and Mattie's.

His time with Mattie was the highlight of her son's week, even more important than the after-school programme he was now happily attending and, for Stevie, any time Josh's path crossed hers at work was definitely a highlight. She'd known that they would both be safe with him but now she was really starting to believe that. To feel completely safe. And she was over that brief flash of attraction to the man, despite how powerful it had been. They were friends, that was all. And they were both invested in Mattie's happiness.

It was a part of good parenting, wasn't it? Letting go a bit? Encouraging independence? Stevie went to the door of Mattie's small bedroom and watched him for a moment as he focused intently on the screen of the tablet he was holding.

'Hey, Matt?'

'Shh, Mum… I'm busy. Gotta open my parachute and find where I'm gonna land on the island.'

'Okay. We can talk later. I was just thinking that maybe you might like to go and visit Gran for a weekend soon and see your old friends. We could think about you going on the bus.'

'By my*self*?' The screen was forgotten.

'Would you like to do that?'

'Yes...' Even the sound of something crashing loudly in the game didn't make Mattie look down again. His face had the same kind of glow that Stevie had seen when she'd gone to that veterinary clinic that day to find him there...with Josh...

And there he was again. In her head. And somewhere deeper than that as well, because even thinking about him created an odd feeling of warmth. Comfort, almost. He was a thread that seemed to be weaving itself throughout every aspect of her life. Even giving Mattie the independence of a bus ride by himself had been Josh's idea. What would happen, Stevie wondered, if that thread got pulled out for whatever reason? Would her life unravel?

Was she trusting Josh too much?

Instinct told her that her trust was not misplaced but it was hard won after so many years of fiercely guarding her own independence as well as protecting her child. If it was just her that was in danger of getting hurt, it wouldn't matter nearly so much, but this was about Mattie and seeing that joy on his face was what mattered more than anything. Maybe it *was* okay that Josh was becoming such an important person in her son's life but there were others that shouldn't be neglected and her mother—Mattie's only grandparent—was top of that list.

'Let's video call Gran when you've finished your game and see what she thinks about the idea.'

Mattie swiped his screen. 'I'm done. Let's call her right now.'

There was always something a bit different about a Saturday morning ward round that Josh Stanmore thoroughly enjoyed. It was more relaxed, possibly because elective surgery only happened on weekdays, consultants were only called in when necessary and the prospect of an afternoon and evening off was a bonus. Less pressure in general gave Josh extra time to spend with the more junior members of his team. It also gave him more time to spend with his patients.

Like thirteen-year-old Fraser who had been admitted with diabetic ketoacidosis recently and was now learning about the impact a diagnosis of Type One diabetes was going to have on his life. A quiet lad, and the oldest of four children, Fraser had impressed Josh no end by not only taking the news in his stride, coping with being alone in hospital much of the time as his single mother had to be home for his younger siblings but also the way he was insisting on learning to test his blood glucose levels and inject his insulin doses himself.

As Josh explained to his senior house officer, Fraser wouldn't be a candidate for an insulin pump until he'd demonstrated how well he could control his blood sugar levels, how consistent his motivation was, how he could manage his diet and whether fluctuations in levels were affecting his schoolwork, sports or day-to-day living. The first priority was to get him stable and well monitored.

'How's it going, Fraser?' Josh perched on the end of the bed.

'It's all good. My level was eight this morning.'

'Have you recorded that in your diary?'

'Yes.'

'When are you due for your insulin?'

'Right about now.' It wasn't Fraser who answered the query, however. It was his nurse who came behind the curtains with a stainless-steel kidney dish containing a syringe and alcohol wipe. She had a bright yellow, portable 'sharps' container in her other hand. 'Want to show the doctor how good you are at doing this, Fraser?'

Seeing Stevie on the ward on a Saturday took Josh by surprise and then he remembered that it was this weekend that Mattie had gone to visit his grandmother. Had Stevie made herself available to cover any gaps in the roster, perhaps? That wasn't what was his overwhelming reaction to seeing her, mind you. No…that was more like how much of a bonus it was that she was here, working in the same space at the same time as him.

So nice, in fact, that it was only now that Josh realised just how important his friendship with Stevie had become over the last weeks. How much he…*liked* her…and trusted her. This was the first time Josh had ever had a friendship with a woman that didn't include sex and, surprisingly, it had advantages he hadn't seen coming. Like knowing that it wasn't going to become something that he needed to walk away from. Like how *safe* it felt.

Fraser clearly liked Stevie as well. It was Stevie that he was looking at for approval as he demonstrated and explained a now well-practised routine.

'So I've taken off both the caps and I dialled up two units so I can get the air out.' Fraser held the insulin pen up and squirted a fine stream of liquid into the air. 'Now I dial up my dose, which is one, and then I can inject it.'

He pinched his stomach, inserted the tiny needle, counting to six before he removed it. 'And that's it. Easy…' He was looking up at Stevie, whose smile told him exactly how well he'd done. How proud she was of him.

Just intercepting that look gave Josh a distinct squeeze in his chest that felt like…longing? As if he wanted to be the person that Stevie was proud of?

Whoa…where the hell had that thought come from?

Josh cleared his throat. 'Well done, Fraser. It's a brave thing to be learning to do by yourself.'

Fraser nodded slowly. 'I *was* scared at first,' he admitted. 'But then Stevie told me that was okay to be scared. And that you could only *be* brave if you did something that you were scared of. Because, if you aren't scared of it, you don't have to be brave, do you?'

For a heartbeat, Josh couldn't think of anything to say to that. Because he'd glanced up and caught Stevie's gaze as Fraser had been speaking. Because he could see that she knew exactly what it was like to be facing something that scared you and how hard it could be to deal with it. He'd told her that he thought she was brave having chosen to face life as a single mother. That wasn't the only thing he'd said, either.

He'd told her that she was both brave *and* beautiful…

And, man…right now she looked more beautiful than any woman he'd ever seen. The highlights of that hair that could catch the light and flicker like firelight and those incredible eyes were there for everybody to see but there was so much more that Josh was aware of. Like her strength and determination. Her ability to defend herself and protect her son. The palpable amount of warmth and care she could offer her patients, like taking the time to have a philosophical discussion with a boy on the brink of adolescence about what it meant to be brave. If someone had told him that when he'd been just a kid, it might have made so many challenges more bearable. It might have made him a much stronger person, in fact.

It was Stevie who broke that brief eye contact. She held out the sharps container for Fraser to drop the needle into and then she shared a smile with her patient and Josh could feel the connection between them. The absolute trust. It was no wonder that Ruby was so impressed with her new member of the paediatric nursing staff. He was impressed himself, having no doubt that Stevie's encouragement and wise words had had a lot to do with how amazingly well Fraser was dealing with a major life change.

Stevie was dealing with one herself today, wasn't she? It had taken courage to let Mattie go off on an adventure by himself to visit his grandmother. Perhaps that was why she'd chosen to work today—so that she had some distraction from knowing how far away her son was?

She was just as focused on one of his last patients to review this morning. Five-year-old Jackson had been treated for hydrocephalus as an infant but the shunt had failed and had been replaced a couple of days ago.

Wearing his new, dinosaur, bicycle helmet, the cheerful boy was ready for discharge and a few adventures of his own but Josh took the time to make sure both Jackson's parents and his junior doctors were fully informed about the recent surgery.

Somehow, it wasn't a surprise to find Stevie in the staffroom later that morning with a neurology textbook open in front of her as she sipped her coffee. Ruby was at the sink, rinsing a plastic container, as Josh reached for a mug and poured himself some of the filter coffee that was always available.

'Saw you over at Cheltenham Central Hospital yesterday, when I was visiting a friend,' Ruby said. 'That's a flash new car you've got.'

'What?' Josh had no idea what she was talking about.

'Silvery thing. What is it? A Porsche? Maserati?'

Josh had to laugh. 'Are you kidding? You really think that's my style?'

'It might be a pretty good chick magnet,' Ruby murmured. She tilted her head towards where Stevie was sitting quietly reading. 'If, you know, nothing else was working. It's a bit strange, you being single for so long now.

It's been months…' She was grinning as she finished drying her container and turned to leave, her voice rising again. 'Good to see that you've had a shave since then, anyway. I don't hold with that designer stubble—it's just laziness in my book.'

Josh shook his head. He still had no idea what Ruby was on about, other than a reference to him and Stevie being more than friends and that wasn't going to happen, was it? Not that he was about to tell Ruby of their connection away from work. He sat down at the table beside Stevie as Ruby left the staffroom.

'You checking up on what I was telling Jackson's parents?'

'Of course not.' The spots of colour on Stevie's cheeks made Josh wonder how long it was since he'd seen a woman blush. 'I just wanted to know more. And I couldn't remember what you'd said about the different sorts of shunts.'

It wasn't just that flush of colour on her face that had captured Josh. He could actually sense her intelligence and the hunger for new knowledge. It was going to be a real pleasure to provide that, although, to be honest, it would be a pleasure just to be sitting here, this close to her.

'Jackson's got a ventriculoperitoneal shunt,' he told her. 'It drains the CSF into his abdomen where it's absorbed into the bloodstream. It's the type of shunt that has fewer risks than, say, a ventriculoatrial shunt that drains it into the right atrium of the heart. Anything else you want to know, just ask.'

'I'll read up on it all properly later.' Stevie glanced at her watch. 'I'd better get back to it now. I think Fraser's mum is bringing his brothers and sister in to see him after lunch so I'll need to clear the decks fast.' She reached for a scrap of paper on the table in front of her to mark the chapter in the book but Josh had seen it first.

'What's this?'

'Just an advertisement I noticed in the paper.'

'It's a cottage in the next village to mine...' Josh picked up the ad and looked at it more closely. 'I saw the sign go up last week. Are you going to have a look at it? Look—there's an open home this afternoon.'

Stevie was taking her mug back to the sink. 'Maybe. I doubt that it's in my price range, though. An eighteenth-century Cotswold cottage with flagstone floors and a walled garden? It'll be worth a fortune.'

'Not necessarily. It obviously needs rethatching and probably even more work inside. Could be a bargain.'

Stevie took the clipping from his hand and closed the textbook around it, as if to finish the conversation, but Josh had seen the flash of something like hope in her eyes. This was her dream, to have a cottage like that, wasn't it? The force of the desire that she could achieve that dream was something else that took Josh by surprise.

'I could come with you,' he offered. 'I know a bit about renovating cottages like that. What time do you finish work?'

'Three o'clock.'

'That would give us just enough time to get there. You don't have to rush home, do you? With Mattie being away?'

She was surprised that he'd remembered. Josh could see that the surprise was about to morph into doubt, which would end up with her probably going home alone to fret about Mattie so he tried to sound as if it was already a done deal.

'I'll be outside the front door at three p.m. Black Jeep, rather old and not very flash, despite what Ruby thinks. You can follow me to the village.' He drained his coffee and stood up. 'You'll be doing me a favour, actually. I'd love an excuse to go and have a look myself. That era of cottages is a bit of a passion of mine.'

It didn't matter that the thatch was covered in moss and so rotten in places the entire roof sagged a bit in the middle. Or that plastered interior walls were crumbling here and there, windows were broken, the kitchen was not much more than an ancient cooktop and a sink with a dripping tap and the small, walled garden hadn't been touched for years.

Stevie could see past all that. Already, in her mind's eye, she was sitting in front of a fire, looking up at restored, exposed beams with the smell of something delicious that was cooking slowly in an Aga that filled up a whole wall of the kitchen. She stood there for so long, for one last look, that the agent picked up his sign and gave them a wave before driving off.

Josh didn't seem to mind standing out here in the cold.

'You're in love with it, aren't you?'

Yes, Stevie could absolutely feel that deliciously intense combination of excitement and anticipation and…the *hope* that came with falling in love. She let her breath out in a happy sigh. 'It's perfect.'

Josh laughed. 'Dunno about that. But it could be really nice. And, despite how bad that thatch looks, it seems weathertight for the moment so you wouldn't have a huge, urgent expense.'

'Mmm…' Stevie took a final glance over her shoulder. 'Did you see that fireplace?'

'An inglenook. I've got one of those. I've put a log burner into the space, which is really practical and looks great. Hey… I'm only five minutes down the road. Come and have a look. It might give you some ideas for your place.'

It was Stevie's turn to laugh. *Her* place? In her dreams.

But dreams were important, she thought as she followed Josh towards where they'd parked their cars down the street. Dreams were soul food. It was why she collected the pictures of gorgeous cottages—so that she could have a little bit of time to escape reality and dream of a future that was everything she could ever want. It was a bit like buying a lotto ticket. Or reading a romance story that had the perfect, happy ending. You knew that it happened to the lucky ones in real life so it wasn't just a fantasy to believe that it could happen to you, and for a few minutes while you indulged in that dream it *was* happening.

What better time to escape reality and dip into a dream just a bit further? If she went home now, she'd probably start worrying about Mattie. Her mother was taking great care of him but he'd gone off to see one of his old school friends this afternoon and he was having tea with his mate's family. She wouldn't even get a text message to reassure her for hours yet.

Had Josh known that? Was that why he had encouraged her to come out to this village to view a property she was unlikely to be able to afford? Why he was offering to give her even more ideas to play with? Her questioning glance was probably quite sharp, which might have been why Josh's eyebrows rose instantly, but then he smiled and Stevie knew that he knew exactly what she'd been thinking. And that she wasn't wrong. He wanted her to dream. To escape. And he was quite happy to go along with it. To be a part of her fantasy, even…

Something twisted deep in her heart right then. A combination of everything she knew about Josh Stanmore, mixed with the poignant feeling that someone cared that much about how she was feeling and, on top of that—like the most delicious icing on a cake—was the renewed awareness of just how gorgeous this man was, with those warm, dark eyes and that, oh, so contagious smile.

It was creeping up on her and she hadn't seen it coming so it hit her with enough force to steal her breath before she'd even finished taking it.

It wasn't just that cottage that Stevie was falling in love with, was it? However intense those feelings were for that ancient cottage, they paled in comparison to what she was feeling at this moment. And yet this man had never kissed her. Never even looked as though he wanted to kiss her so where on earth had this wash of overwhelming emotion sprung from?

Perhaps it could be traced back to the relief she'd seen in his eyes when he'd saved the life of that little girl who'd come very close to choking to death. Or maybe it was the way he often made her feel so proud of her own work?

Was it the respect he'd shown when he'd made sure they were in the private space of the rooftop garden before talking about anything personal? Or was it because he'd won the trust of her son and herself and become such a special part of their lives?

Or maybe this had been enough on its own—that he was prepared to step into her dream and make it far more real than it could have ever been otherwise. Yeah... Stevie's steps slowed as they reached their vehicles. She could love someone just for that.

Mix that warm, fuzzy appreciation with the sheer masculine attraction this man exuded and the combination was a sexual timebomb. One that she could simply not allow to explode. But one that she didn't seem to have quite enough willpower to walk away from, either. Not that that was necessarily a problem, a small voice whispered in the back of her mind, because this extraordinary awareness was one-sided, wasn't it?

She should still go home, though. To her home, not his. Stevie opened her mouth to thank Josh for the offer and excuse herself but something quite different came out. 'I'd love to see your cottage,' she told him. 'I'll follow you again, shall I?'

Stevie was laughing again and it made Josh's grin widen even though he knew she was laughing at him. Or maybe she was just enjoying the exuberant welcome she was getting from Lucky as she stooped to pet the little terrier as he shot outside the moment the front door was opened.

But she was shaking her head as she straightened. 'You're really calling this a *cottage*?'

'There's its name, right there, beside the door. "Weeping Elm Cottage". Named after that tree that takes up most of the front garden. It's a good thing there's a bit of a meadow out the back or there'd be no room for Lucky to have a run around. He's almost lost his limp now.'

'It's not a cottage. It's a mansion.'

'You haven't seen the estates that are tucked away in the forests around here. This is just a slightly bigger version of your cottage. Four bedrooms instead of two, that's all.' Josh held the door open for her. 'Come on in.'

He couldn't wait to see her face when he

showed her his home. He wanted to see that spark of interest in her eyes that was intense enough to be more like passion as it lit up her whole face. It was intriguing to see it in something that had nothing to do with work. Or Mattie. What else did Stevie Hawksbury feel passionate about other than very old houses? What else could make her laugh because he would really love to hear that again.

His front door opened directly into his living room, with its whitewashed walls, rough-hewn beams, window seats beneath the multipaned windows, wide elm floorboards and the eye-catching centrepiece of a dramatic, stone-built inglenook fireplace. Lucky trotted ahead of them as if he, too, was excited about showing Stevie their home.

Stevie's face didn't just light up, she looked almost overwhelmed, standing very still—her eyes wide and her lips slightly parted—turning her head very slowly to take it all in. Josh couldn't take his eyes off her face. Especially that wayward, tight curl that had fallen across her forehead to almost tangle itself in her eyelashes. And the unconscious drift of her lips that made it look as though she was about to be kissed.

*Good grief…*that thought was enough

to be stirring something in his gut that he hadn't seen coming. Something totally inappropriate given that definitive brush-off Stevie had given him the first day he'd met her. Fortunately, Josh caught a movement from the corner of his eye that made him turn his head.

'Off the sofa, Lucky,' he commanded. 'We've talked about this before, haven't we?'

Lucky jumping down was enough to break that stillness for Stevie. She was moving further away from him—towards the fireplace.

'This mantlepiece...' She stepped onto the flagstone hearth to reach up and touch the massive beam of wood that was embedded in the wall. 'It looks like a whole tree trunk. It's incredible. How old *is* your house?'

'Dates to about mid-eighteenth century, I believe. The wood burner doesn't look too out of place, though, does it?'

'It's gorgeous. And I love how you can stack the logs on either side like that. Did the flue from the log burner just go inside the original chimney?'

She was leaning in to peer up into the space and Josh didn't think to warn her not to touch the inside of the chimney. It hadn't occurred to him that there could still be some ancient soot clinging to stonework until Stevie straightened and pushed that curl back off her face, leaving a huge, black streak in its place.

'Oh, no…'

'What? Have I got something on my face?' Stevie was touching her nose now, and then her cheek and then she saw her fingers and laughed.

'Don't move…' Josh walked past the fireplace to where the living room led into his kitchen. He grabbed a clean tea towel, ran it under the tap and went back to Stevie who used it to wipe her hands and then her face.

'Have I got it all?'

'Almost.'

Without thinking, Josh reached out and used the pad of his thumb to wipe a remnant of smudge from her cheek. Close to her mouth. So close, he could feel the corners of her lips. And how incredibly soft her skin was… It was his turn to stop in his tracks, suddenly overwhelmed with what he could feel. And see. The way Stevie's gaze was locked on his, the way those gloriously tawny eyes darkened and…oh, man…the way her lips had parted again. And this time, he just knew that she *was* waiting to be kissed.

That she *wanted* to be kissed.

It was obviously the day for not thinking things through. He hadn't warned her about the soot. He hadn't hesitated in touching her face but maybe, this time, he just didn't want to let anything stop him responding to an invitation that promised him something he might deeply regret missing out on if he didn't accept it.

By the time his head had dipped—oh, so slowly—far enough for his lips to be hovering just above Stevie's there was no turning back. Not when she was coming up on her toes to close that final fraction of space between them. And certainly not when he could feel the soft, delicious responsiveness of her lips beneath his.

This was the kiss he'd been waiting for his entire life.

He just hadn't known it even existed.

He could feel Stevie melting in his arms as he deepened that kiss and time slowed to a point where it felt like this dance of touch and taste and sensation was as familiar as breathing. When it stopped being too much and became not enough but then instantly became too much again as Stevie pulled abruptly out of his arms.

Her breath was coming in short gasps but she still pressed her hand against her mouth. 'Oh, no…' Her tone was far less amused than his had been when he'd used those exact words when he'd seen the sooty smudges on her face. She sounded—and looked—horrified. 'That should *not* have happened.'

'No…' Josh's agreement was rather half-hearted despite knowing, deep down, that she was quite right. But it *had* happened and he wasn't exactly sorry. Clearly, he hadn't quite come to his senses again yet because what he actually wanted was for it to happen again.

And, judging by the fact that Stevie actually looked like she might be about to burst into tears—which was a bit scary given that he knew how strong a person she was—an opportunity to kiss her again wasn't going to happen any time soon.

CHAPTER FIVE

DON'T CRY, STEVIE ordered herself. *Don't you dare cry...*

But this felt a bit like that day she'd first met Josh all those weeks ago, when she'd gone to hide in that supply room and buried her face in her hands, convinced that she'd ruined what had held the promise of a wonderful new start in life.

There was nowhere to go to hide now. She couldn't even hide how she was feeling with the way Josh was holding her gaze like this. This wasn't the first time that Stevie had thought that he understood her way better than anyone else ever had and, coming in the wake of that astonishing kiss, she knew she really *was* in danger of bursting into tears.

'Hey...' His voice was soft. Gentle. 'It's not that bad, Stevie.' Josh was actually smiling as he put his arms around her to offer her a hug. 'It was just a kiss.'

Really?

It was impossible not to respond to the comfort of his arms around her body or to stop herself pressing her face into the soft wool of his jumper, in that dip below his shoulder that was just made for shielding someone from the world. But...*just* a kiss? Stevie had never experienced a kiss like that. It still felt as if her world had tilted on its axis so sharply she'd been on the point of falling into space.

'It's a disaster.'

Her voice was muffled. Then she could feel as well as hear the amused sound Josh was making so she lifted her head to make sure he could hear her clearly.

'Mattie's going to hate me. Probably for ever.'

'Why?' Josh pulled back far enough to be able to see her face.

'You must realise what would happen if the Big Brother organisation found out I'd kissed my son's mentor. It probably breaks all the rules and he'd never be allowed to see you again and...and he's been happier just lately than he's been in a very long time.'

Josh was frowning. 'How on earth are they going to find out? Besides, I think it was me who kissed you, not the other way round.'

The implication of those words went straight over Stevie's head because she had too much else to think about. 'But *we* know. What if Mattie found out?'

'Mattie's not here,' Josh said calmly. 'The only person other than us who knows about that kiss is Lucky.'

Hearing his name, the little dog sat up, his head on one side, his tail wagging.

'It's about time for your dinner, isn't it?' Josh said. He looked down at Stevie and smiled. 'How 'bout I make us a cup of tea at the same time and we can talk about this like grown-ups. Like friends? It really isn't the end of the world.'

It really *wasn't* the end of the world.

It just felt like it.

But it wasn't until Stevie was curled up on one end of the soft, feather-filled cushions of Josh's sofa in front of the log burner he had fired up to show her what it was like when it was going, and they'd been sticking to neutral topics and had been chatting about renovating old houses and the cup of tea had been replaced by a particularly nice glass of wine, that she realised *why*.

It wasn't that she was upset by the fact that they had kissed at all.

What was actually devastating was that they couldn't let it go any further when every cell in Stevie's body was aching for more…

Josh was sitting at the other end of the couch and somehow Lucky had sneaked up to occupy the middle. The little dog was stretched out on his back now, looking for all the world as if he was sunbathing somewhere on a Mediterranean beach.

'He looks so happy,' Stevie said. 'And he's so cute. I can't believe his owners haven't come looking for him.'

'Animals get dumped for all sorts of reasons.' Josh swirled the last bit of wine in the bottom of his glass. 'So do people.' He drained the glass and reached for the bottle on the coffee table to refill it.

Stevie blinked at the dark undercurrent that three simple little words could generate.

'Sorry…' Josh sat back against the cushions and closed his eyes. After a long moment, however, he opened them again to look directly at Stevie. 'What is it about you,' he asked quietly, 'that makes me say things I'd never say to anyone else? *Ever?*'

Stevie couldn't answer that. Even if she could have found the words, they probably wouldn't have come out given that squeeze in her chest that was taking her breath away. She'd never felt this close to anyone and it was far more than something purely physical. This felt like being touched on a far deeper level. One that was all about trust. And love...

'You did tell me,' she said softly, 'that you were adopted and then they changed their minds. I can't believe anyone would do something like that.'

'I got dumped the day I was born,' Josh said into the silence that followed Stevie's words. 'I believe I was in a foster home for a while and then I got adopted by an older couple—Colin and Judith Stanmore. They'd been trying to have their own children for twenty years by then and my mother was nearly forty.'

Stevie took a sip of her wine. Josh wasn't looking at her as he spoke quietly but she couldn't take her eyes off his face. Off those lines beside his eyes and lips that could deepen and light up his face when he smiled but, for now, just made him look serious enough to appear unbearably sad. Off the way he rubbed at the back of his neck when he was deciding whether to say something difficult.

'It was one of "those" stories,' Josh continued. 'You know, when people finally adopt a child and then this miracle happens and they discover that they can have their own child, after all. That happened when I was about three and my earliest memory was my parents bringing him home from the hospital. I'd never seen them so happy. I was happy. Any photos from that time made us look like the perfect little family.'

'What happened?' Stevie encouraged softly. 'What changed?'

'Derek was their "real" son.' Josh took a long sip of his wine. 'Oh, I think they tried their best but it became a burden that I needed attention as well. I heard them, one night, talking about how it would be best to find me a new family but who would want me now that I wasn't a cute baby any more? And I was becoming so badly behaved.'

Stevie's breath came out in an incredulous huff. 'I wonder why that was?' she muttered,

her heart breaking for the small boy who had been so desperate to be noticed. To be loved.

'The crunch came when Derek got sick one night. They both rushed him off to the hospital and I don't think it even occurred to them that they shouldn't have left me alone in the house. The police found me wandering down the street the next day, looking for them, and it was my grandmother who came to get me. My parents didn't want me back and she was so furious with them she took me home with her, even though she was well into her seventies and raising a child was the last thing she really wanted to do.'

Josh reached for the wine bottle to refill Stevie's glass this time. 'Sorry…not sure why I'm dumping this on you. Maybe it's a very long-winded way of explaining why I'm not about to abandon Lucky. Or why I felt drawn to get involved with the Big Brother programme, perhaps. The first thing I though when I looked at that brochure was how go it might have been to have someone like t in my life.'

'What happened later? Did your pa ever apologise?'

'Never saw them again. Grandma spoke to them after that. She just did

and brought me up as best she could. She died while I was away at medical school. Her son and his family didn't come to her funeral or even contest her will, which was a surprise given that she'd left her house and everything to me.' Josh pulled in a deep breath. 'I think that was the final point of my journey in giving up on the idea of families. I decided that I didn't need one. Or want one.' He raised his glass. 'Friends, however, are entirely different. Here's to you and me, Stevie.'

She had to lean over Lucky to touch her glass to his.

So…she certainly knew why he lived alone now. But how sad was that—to never want a family because he'd been so unlucky with his own? And how heroic was it to have devoted his life to helping save the lives of other people's children, so that other families could stay together if at all possible?

'Oh…' Josh lowered his glass after taking a sip. 'I know where all that came from. I just wanted to reassure you that nothing's really changed, I guess. That I made a promise to the universe when I took on being Mattie's mentor that I would never do anything to break the trust he was giving me

because…because I know how much damage that can do.'

Didn't he just? Enough damage that Josh was never going to trust in family again. Enough that he was never going to do anything to hurt her son.

'Thank you.' Stevie's smile started out a bit wobbly but slowly grew. She had to blink a couple of times, too, just in case there was an errant tear hiding somewhere.

'That doesn't mean I can't be friends with Mattie's mum,' Josh added. 'But it does mean that you're in the same category. You've trusted me and I'm not going to break that trust.'

She believed him. In spite of that kiss that had just turned her world upside down she knew that Josh would never intentionally hurt her. Or maybe it was partly because of that kiss. Because nobody could kiss you that tenderly, as if you were the most important person in the universe, unless he genuinely cared.

Oh, man…

Stevie had never looked this gorgeous. Maybe it was because there were actual flames flickering in the background and those wild curls had been released from whatever ties tried to tame them during working hours and they were touching her shoulders and creating a kind of halo that picked up on every flicker of the burning wood in the fire in the rapidly fading daylight. He should get up and put a lamp on but he was enjoying watching her too much.

And *that* was probably because he still hadn't come to his senses completely. His brain had been doing its best—it had even dredged up ancient history that should have put paid to any fantasy moment—but his body hadn't got with the programme yet. He could still feel what it had been like to touch Stevie. To taste her...

He still wanted more.

More distraction was needed. Something professional might help. Josh waved his hand at the massive bookshelf that lined the wall behind the sofa.

'I've got a small library of textbooks here, in case you hadn't noticed. If you ever want to read up on something—like hydrocephalus, perhaps—just let me know.'

Stevie nodded. 'I'd love to do some more training. I had a lot of catching up to do before I could get back to working in a proper hospital but I want to do more. I've lost a lot of years. Not that I regret it,' she added hastily. 'And working in aged care was the only sort of nursing with hours that fitted well enough around school and childcare but I'm loving getting back to paediatrics.'

'Is that where you worked before Mattie came along?'

Stevie nodded. 'It was always where I wanted to be. I couldn't believe my luck when I got a job at one of London's best paediatric hospitals. And I thought I'd met the perfect man on my first day at work. It was a dream come true.' She drank the last of her wine. 'Until it wasn't, of course.'

Josh heard the sigh of that broken dream. The broken trust. It made his own heart ache.

'I still thought it would be okay,' Stevie said softly. 'I thought he loved me. That we'd end up in that little house with a picket fence and we'd be that perfect little family. How naive was that?'

'You trusted the bastard,' Josh growled. 'Who was he? Some playboy medical student?'

'Um…' There was a gleam of amusement in Stevie's eyes. 'He was a consultant. Pretty much my boss, I guess.'

Josh could actually feel his stomach sinking like a stone. 'Oh… *God*… And then I go and hit on you the first day we met.'

Stevie dropped her gaze, giving her head a tiny shake. 'You weren't hitting on me,' she said. 'I just overreacted. You were trying to be welcoming to a new staff member. I get that now.'

'No…' Josh swallowed hard when the silence had gone on a little too long. 'I'm not going to lie to you, Stevie. I kind of *was* hitting on you.'

He heard the sharp intake of her breath as her gaze flicked up to meet his. He could also see her eyes darken again—the way they had just before he'd kissed her and, man… did that mess with his head, not to mention other parts of his anatomy?

One corner of his mouth tried to curl into an apologetic smile but it didn't quite work.

'I couldn't resist,' he admitted. 'There you were, the most gorgeous woman I'd ever seen, and you'd just demonstrated the fact that you were also highly intelligent, extremely good at your job and that you were strong and brave enough not to crack under the intense pressure of a life or death situation. You blew me away, Stevie.' It was his turn to shake his head. 'You still do.' This time, he did find a gentle smile. 'It was a good thing you knocked me back, though. You deserve someone who can give you far more than I could have.'

'Oh?' The look she was giving him had enough heat to be melting something deep inside his gut. 'Such as…?'

'The possibility of a future,' Josh said. 'Commitment. The kind of thing I can never offer and, even though I've always made it clear that I can't right from the start of anything, I know I've hurt a lot of women by not being able to give them what they wanted.'

'That's not your fault.' Stevie was still staring at him. 'I understand why you feel the way you do and if you're always as honest about that as you've been with me, then you're not breaking any promises. Or trust. People only get hurt when they expect—or want—something that they thought existed that then gets taken away from them.'

There was something that Stevie wasn't saying. Josh couldn't decide what it was, exactly—was it too much to hope that she might be telling him that he wouldn't have hurt her by offering her a 'friendship with benefits' because she wouldn't have expected anything more than that? That she wasn't actually looking for a long-term commitment from any man because she had her life sorted perfectly well enough already? He had to clear his throat before he could say anything else and, even then, the words came out in a low kind of growl.

'What is it that *you* want, Stevie?'

'I want to know that Mattie's safe.' Her words were no more than a whisper.

'He is.' It was a vow. 'So are you.'

'We are good at keeping secrets, aren't we?'

'We are.' Josh held Stevie's gaze and it felt as if he was pulling her closer and closing that gap between them. 'And that kiss can always be a secret if that's what you want.'

'What do *you* want?'

Josh could feel a smile trying to escape. 'It's kind of more what I *don't* want.'

'Which is?'

'To spend the rest of my life wondering— if just a kiss could be that mind blowing— what would it be like, even just once, to *really* make love to you?'

Oh…the way the electricity in the air between them reached a point where you could almost hear it sizzling. And the way Stevie's tongue appeared to touch her lip like that as she struggled to find any words in response. It was all Josh could do not to lean in and close that distance between them instantly. But this had to be her choice. Maybe he did lean a little, because Lucky stirred and slid off the couch to go and lie down with a disgruntled thump by the fireplace. Stevie didn't seem to have noticed.

'Just once?'

'Just us,' Josh murmured. 'Just tonight.'

Stevie's eyes closed for a heartbeat. 'A secret?'

'You said it yourself. We're good at secrets.' He was so close to her now. How the heck had that happened? When Stevie opened her eyes, she was going to see that he was close enough to kiss her.

Or maybe she felt it and moved herself. Because Josh was quite sure he hadn't leaned any closer but he could feel the warmth of her breath against his lips.

'I know what I want.' The words were no more than a sigh.

'What's that?'

'You...'

Josh had to take a very deliberate, slow breath to steady himself before he gave in to the overwhelming need to kiss Stevie again. To scoop her into his arms and carry her to his bed.

To give her everything he had to give her of himself.

Because if it was only going to be once, he was going to make sure that neither of them would ever forget this night.

CHAPTER SIX

'WHAT'S WITH THE hairy roof, Mum?'

'It's a thatched roof, Mattie. It's old and special.'

'Looks like it's going bald.'

'Yeah…it's going to need some fixing up. Let's go inside.'

'Why?'

'I told you. It's the last open home before it gets sold this week and I wanted you to see it.'

'Because you're going to buy it?'

'I hope so.'

Stevie lowered her voice as a couple went past them to go through the gate, not wanting anyone to hear any note of confidence in her voice, but it really did look as if things were coming together after weeks of effort. Her mother was providing a deposit from the 'rainy day' shares her father had put aside years ago and the bank was on board for a mortgage. Her limit for bidding in the auction was strict but she had to be in with a shout given how much work the cottage needed.

She clearly wasn't the only person seriously interested, however. Judging by the effusive welcome from the smartly dressed estate agent waiting to greet the couple ahead of Stevie and Mattie at the front door, this wasn't their first visit to the property. Turning her head, she glanced at the late model European car parked behind her reliable but rather old hatchback and it felt like her dream might be developing some slippery patches as she tried to hang onto it but that just made Stevie even more determined. She'd won battles before and this was definitely worth fighting for.

'It's got a garden,' she told Mattie, brightly. 'Just a little one, but there's a village green not far down the road with plenty of room to ride a bike or kick a ball around.'

The mention of the garden seemed to have given Mattie a reason to get far more interested in this weekend outing. 'So this would be a *real* house, then? *Our* house?'

Stevie nodded and couldn't help her smile

turning into a grin. Because she could see the way Mattie's face lit up with that kind of glow she had been seeing more and more recently—especially when he'd been out for his weekly session with Josh and Lucky. She could feel a very similar glow herself quite often these days and that also had a lot to do with having a session of her own with Josh.

Once would never have been enough, would it?

Not when the physical chemistry she and Josh seemed to have together was enough to stop the earth turning for a significant length of time. When even *thinking* about the touch of his fingers, or his tongue or of her touching him could make something in Stevie's gut ignite with a heat so intense it was painful.

'So this is the living room. Look at that fireplace.'

Stevie had had to learn the new skill of finding something else to focus on very fast when that heat threatened to melt any rational thought and she'd become very good at it because she'd had no other option. She had to work with Josh, after all, and going weak at the knees was simply not acceptable.

And she had to keep their secret from everybody. From her colleagues, including Ruby who had a well-honed radar for any shenanigans going on in her patch between staff members but, so far, she didn't seem to have picked up on any glances that lingered a little too long, that Stevie and Josh often shared a rooftop lunch, and that their rosters might have been juggled to give them the same days off more often than not.

It was a secret Stevie had to keep from her son, too, and, like most children, he had an uncanny ability to pick up on things that weren't being said. He was staring at her now, with a somewhat bewildered expression on his face.

'You really like this place, don't you, Mum?'

'I love it,' she whispered. 'But don't tell anybody.'

'Why not?' Mattie whispered back.

Stevie tilted her head towards where the real estate agent was talking to the couple in the kitchen. 'When people use an auction to sell a house, it's kind of a competition,' she explained. 'And it's better not to let the others know what you're thinking.'

Especially when it involved X-rated memories, like the one that came from nowhere as Stevie took her gaze away from that in-glenook fireplace, thinking that it needed a lot of work to look anything like the one in Josh's house, which led to a flashback to that first time together that was so vivid Stevie had to bite her lip quite hard to distract her-self this time. They hadn't managed another night together since that weekend Mattie had been away but... *Oh, my...* Some of their af-ternoons when they both had a day off and Mattie was at school... Stevie could actually feel a blush warming her cheeks.

But Mattie clearly hadn't noticed anything amiss. He was smiling at her, in fact.

'What?' Stevie smiled back. 'What are you thinking?'

'About Josh.'

Stevie blinked. 'Oh?'

'It was something he said. About when we didn't have to live in that apartment any more. When we had a *proper* house?' His smile stretched into a grin. 'He said that Lucky could come and live with me.' The smile faded too fast then. 'But that was a long time ago. Do you think he might have changed his mind?'

'I wouldn't think so. Josh isn't the kind

of man who would change his mind about something important.'

Stevie certainly knew that much about Josh—that he was completely trustworthy. And honest. When they'd both realised that not ever repeating that one-off, *amazing* night was going to drive them both completely insane, they'd both made a promise that it was never going to affect Mattie. And that if this overwhelming attraction between them fizzled out, they would make sure it didn't destroy their friendship or do any damage to Josh's relationship with Mattie.

Okay…so maybe it was a bit more than friendship on Stevie's part but she was confident she could handle this 'friends with benefits' thing. The trick was to focus on the present and not try and imagine a future that involved any dreaming about things that might never happen because that was the way to avoid getting your heart broken. If a friendship with Josh was all that was ever going to happen between them, she would make the most of everything it brought into her life.

She was applying the same strategy to what this cottage represented as the potential home she was in love with. She was focusing on only what was happening now and the need to succeed in the auction this week. It was possible she might never be able to afford the kind of renovations that would make it perfect but just living here would be enough and she would make the most of everything that it could bring into both her life and Mattie's.

Mattie wasn't looking convinced by her optimism about whether Josh would keep his promise, however.

'Talk to Josh about it, next time you see him.'

'But that's not for days and days.'

'He doesn't live so far from here.' Stevie spoke without really thinking. 'Maybe we could go and say hello to Lucky on the way home.'

'Is that allowed? When it's not our usual day?'

'It's probably bending the rules a bit,' Stevie admitted.

'And how do you know where he lives?'

It was easy enough to shrug off the awkward question. 'Josh and I work together, remember? We're friends, too.'

It could be stepping over the boundaries they had clearly marked in the different ways their lives connected, though, so it might be a good idea to think it through a bit better. 'I can text him,' she told Mattie. 'And make sure he's home.'

The real estate agent and the other couple were coming back into the living room. 'Why don't you go upstairs and look at the bedrooms?' Stevie suggested. 'I need to ask a couple of questions about the auction.' To register her interest, in fact, though she was going to wait until she could speak to the agent alone.

'I don't know, darling.' The man was frowning. 'It needs an awful lot of work. Like totally gutting the place. And getting rid of that fireplace.'

'Ah…' The agent's smile was cautious. 'This is a Grade Two listed property.'

'What does that mean?' The blonde woman was a lot younger than Stevie. Was she his daughter or his girlfriend?

'It means it's legally protected from being demolished, extended or significantly altered without special permission.'

'It means a nightmare from what I've heard,' her partner added. 'You have to get permission for anything you want to do to the place like changing a tap and it can take months. Years, even.'

'Oh…' The woman pouted. 'But this place is so *cute*.'

The man sighed. 'All we want is a weekend bolthole from London,' he told the agent. 'But if Autumn's got her heart set on this place, we'll have to at least think about it. As long as the price is right, of course.'

If he could afford a car like the one parked in the lane, he could probably buy this cottage without even worrying about a mortgage. Stevie could feel her optimism taking a huge dive. Enough to create fear, even. Then she overheard the man as he left, telling the agent that they had more properties to view, hope soared back again and the roller coaster was starting to do Stevie's head in.

She needed support, she decided, and she only had one really good friend available in her new life. One who, coincidentally, lived just down the road. What would happen if she just turned up on his doorstep, unannounced, with Mattie in tow? If nothing else, it would certainly let her know if she was right to trust him as much as she did.

And…she couldn't help the bubble of something else surfacing. The hope that she might see that there was something else she could trust? That what she and Josh had found together might actually be enough to change his mind one day. That he might come to believe—like she did—that family was really the most important thing you could find in life?

For a moment, Josh was stunned by the unexpectedness of finding Stevie and Mattie on his doorstep. It felt like planets were colliding when they weren't supposed to be even be in the same orbit.

But then Lucky launched himself at Mattie with a joyous bark and Mattie dropped to a crouch to cuddle the little dog, which left Josh and Stevie looking at each other and he could see that she was apprehensive.

'We were just down the road,' she told him. 'At the last open house for that cottage. You know, the one I told you about at work?'

There was something more than apprehension in her eyes. A plea of some sort? Josh wasn't sure what it was but he *was* absolutely sure that he would oblige if it was at all possible. Because he wanted to see Stevie smile. Because *her* happiness made *him* happy. And suddenly that made it feel perfectly okay that she was on his doorstep. That she—and Mattie—could be part of any aspect of his life. Quite apart from a sexual relationship of a kind he'd never had in his life before, he and Stevie were friends and they'd both sworn that nothing was going to change that. If this was some kind of test of that friendship, he knew he could pass it with flying colours.

'Come in,' he invited. 'Tell me all about it. I'll make us a cup of tea. Mattie, bring Lucky back inside. You can go and play with him in the back garden, if you want. There's lots more space out there and you'll find a few tennis balls hiding in the grass. Lucky's very good at playing fetch and the vet says it's good for his leg to get a bit more exercise now.'

But Mattie didn't head straight for the meadow out the back. He followed the adults into the kitchen and Josh couldn't miss the significant look that Stevie gave her son, clearly encouraging him to say something.

'What's up, buddy?'

The squeeze that happened in his chest when Mattie looked up to meet his gaze had become very familiar for Josh. The connection he'd felt with this boy right from that first meeting had grown into something very solid that only became stronger whenever they spent time together. He cared very much about Mattie and very much wanted to be a part of his life for many years to come.

'You know what you said about Lucky that time? That if me and Mum got a proper house one day, Lucky could come and live with me?'

Josh nodded gravely. 'I do. And I remember saying that it would be up to your mum to say yes.'

Mattie turned that desperate gaze onto his mother. 'You will, won't you, Mum?'

'If we get the cottage, of course I will,' Stevie promised. 'But remember that it might not happen this time, Mattie. It could be that we'll have to keep looking for another house.'

'Like this one.' Mattie's smile was bright. 'I really like your house, Josh. Come on, Lucky, let's go outside.'

Josh reached for a teapot and some mugs. 'When's the auction?'

'Wednesday. One o'clock.'

'My afternoon off.' He winked at Stevie. 'I'll come with you, shall I? And then we can celebrate afterwards.'

'Oh, I hope so…'

The way Stevie's eyes were shining as they held his gaze gave Josh an even bigger squeeze than his connection with Mattie ever created. It was the thought of getting the house of her dreams that was making her glow like that, of course, but maybe a part of it was the thought of just how they *could* celebrate afterwards when they had the rest of the afternoon to themselves. He made a mental note to put some champagne on ice.

It was all he could do not to reach for Stevie right now, in fact, and pull her into his arms. To lace his fingers through those delicious curls tumbling to her shoulders so that he could hold her head steady as he kissed her completely senseless.

And it was obvious that she knew exactly what he was thinking about. The way she caught the corner of her bottom lip between her teeth was a dead giveaway so it was probably just as well that Mattie chose that moment to come back into the kitchen.

'I'm hungry,' he announced.

'I've got biscuits.' Josh let his gaze hold Stevie's for just another heartbeat before he turned away. 'I might even be able to find a chocolate one.'

Mattie was silent for a moment. He looked at his mother and then at Josh.

'Is Mum your girlfriend?' he asked.

They both laughed. They both said 'no' at precisely the same time—as if the very idea was ridiculous.

'But she's your friend, isn't she?' Mattie persisted.

'Absolutely,' Josh agreed.

'And we work together,' Stevie added.

Mattie ignored his mother's comment. He was still watching Josh. 'And she's a girl.'

Josh laughed again as he held out the biscuit tin towards Mattie. 'Can't argue with that.'

He didn't dare catch Stevie's gaze. He had to slam a mental door, as well, to stop a rush of pure sensation that was determined to remind him of exactly how feminine Stevie was and how much he loved every aspect of that gorgeous body of hers.

Mattie simply nodded, apparently satisfied. Then he took two biscuits and ran outside again with Lucky staying close.

Josh turned his attention to making the tea. 'Let's talk strategy for the auction,' he suggested. 'Are you going to be the first to bid, or hang back until it's slowing down and scare the competition off by making your bid then, as if you're just getting started?'

'I don't know,' Stevie said. 'But I'm worried about the people I saw there today. Older guy with a young blonde who want a weekend "bolthole" from London. I'm really hoping they'll find something they like better so they won't even be there.'

They were there.

Josh recognised the couple from Stevie's description. They were standing near the front of the crowded room the real estate firm was using for their auctions that day. He thought Stevie had a good chance of being successful, with both the pre-approved mortgage she had sourced and the help her mother was providing but she was looking nervous, which made him very pleased that he was here to offer some moral support. He liked the way she was standing so close to him, too—as if she really appreciated that he was here. Or maybe she was taking advantage of the freedom not to have to resist that extraordinary magnetic attraction their bodies seemed to have for each other.

When the bidding started, however, she moved away to stand alone, as if she needed to focus on fighting for her personal dream. For herself and for her son. Josh could see just how much it meant to her by her focus and a tension that he was finding contagious. This was beyond important. This was the dream of a future that simply meant everything to her.

Stevie had been right in thinking that the couple up the front were her main competition. They came straight back with a new bid every time she raised her hand and it was getting closer and closer to the limit Josh knew could not be passed. The other couple were slowing down, taking that bit longer each time before outbidding Stevie so when she nodded to take the amount offered to her limit, Josh held his breath. He could feel his heart pounding against his ribs so heaven only knew how Stevie was feeling at this moment.

And then it happened. Another bid from the bolthole couple took the price several thousand pounds over her limit and Stevie went as white as a sheet. The urge to put his arms around her to offer her his strength was overwhelming but Josh couldn't move a muscle and his brain was racing past that first reaction.

He was thinking of Mattie. Of when he'd started to win the trust of a boy who had been struggling to find his feet in a new life. Of how Mattie had been almost in tears because he'd thought Josh might give Lucky away and how desperately he was hoping that he'd be able to live with the little dog he loved so much when he and Stevie had their own house.

It had to be this house.

But the auctioneer had his gavel poised in the air. 'Going…going…'

In the split second before he could say 'gone', Josh could remember the look on Stevie's face when she'd fallen in love with this cottage. And he could feel the way it had made *him* feel at the time to see her glowing—as if he would be quite prepared to gift wrap the whole world and present it to her if it would make her look that happy all over again.

Because…because he loved her, dammit.

And she deserved to have her dream.

He didn't put his hand up in that pregnant pause before the auctioneer declared the cottage sold. He didn't even shout out the amount that was ten thousand pounds more than the last bid. He spoke loudly, to make sure he was heard, but calmly and confidently enough to advertise that he was just getting started here. And it worked. The bolt-hole couple was stunned into silence until the older man shook his head. Stevie looked just as stunned when the gavel came down with no further bids. There was no hint of joy on her face, though, as the crowd dispersed.

'Why did you *do* that?' Her voice was low. And fierce.

'I didn't want you to lose the cottage. You *or* Mattie.'

'So *you* bought it? You bought the house *I* wanted?'

'No... I made sure you could buy it.' Somehow this gift of assistance was going all wrong and Josh had no idea how to fix it. Unless... Was it her pride that was hurt? Or had he threatened the independence she'd fought so hard for? 'It can just be a loan,' he added. 'With no pressure to pay it back anytime soon. It's only ten thousand pounds.'

'*Only?*'

'We'll work it out. Trust me.'

The agent was smiling as he walked towards Josh. 'Congratulations, sir...' He gestured to indicate a small side room where there was a table and some chairs. 'If you'd like to come with me, we've got a bit of paperwork to sort out here.'

It was only then that Josh realised there could be complications from his impulsive actions. Was he legally responsible for purchasing this property for himself now? It would have to be sorted before the paperwork got completed but there was something more important to sort out first.

'Just give us a minute, please,' he ordered the agent.

Then he grabbed Stevie's hand and took her with him into the privacy of that side room and pushed the door closed behind them.

'Think about it for a minute,' he urged her. 'I know it was a bit crazy but I had to try and help, because...because...' The words died on his tongue as he realised what he had been about to add.

Because I think I might be falling in love with you...

Whoa... Where had that come from?

It's okay, he told himself. *Of course I care about Stevie. We're friends, aren't we?*

'Because of Mattie,' he said aloud. 'We both know how much he wants to live with Lucky. This way he can. And he'll be well away from that gang of boys who've been bullying him and...' Josh managed to find a smile because it felt like he'd reached a much safer space now. 'And we'll never be short of something to do on our Big Brother sessions. There's so much I can teach him about renovation stuff and using tools...it's enough to keep us busy for ever.'

His smile seemed to be reaching inside himself as much as out towards Stevie. He could see himself teaching Mattie to use a hammer or how to plaster a hole in a wall. He could see Stevie helping as well, and Lucky probably getting underfoot and in the way and they'd all pitch in to throw a meal together at the end of a day's work on the cottage. A barbecue, maybe? Or soup and toast in front of the fire.

Kind of like a family but so much safer because it was only about being friends. Because that was something that could be trusted to last so much longer. For ever, even, perhaps?

The shock of what Josh had done by placing the winning bid on the cottage was starting to wear off as Stevie stood there listening to him explaining why he'd done it.

And, creeping through the mist of what had felt like a direct attack on the independence she'd fought to maintain for so long, there was something else that Stevie could feel. A trickle of excitement. The promise of a kind of happiness that she'd always known was out there but had always seemed just out of reach for herself.

It wasn't just that she was about to sign the paperwork that would make her the owner of the house of her dreams.

It was more that she could hear something in Josh's words that he probably had no idea he was saying. She could actually see him spending time with Mattie and working on what would be endless projects for years to come in that little house and garden. They'd be fixing things and painting and digging in the garden and she'd be there. Lucky would be there.

Just like a family.

And maybe…just maybe…that was the real reason Josh had done what he'd just done. He might not know it, and Stevie wouldn't dream of even hinting at it, but she couldn't help feeling that, deep down, Josh actually did want a family.

That tiny flash of fantasy had suggested

something else as well. That maybe she had been wrong to be so convinced that she didn't need a man in her life. That she might actually be able to see a future that would be so much better if she had a soulmate to share it with. It couldn't be just any man, of course. The thought had only occurred to her because it was Josh she'd seen as a part of her life in this cottage.

It was only this man that she could trust enough to love. This man that—even if he never wanted more from her than friendship—felt like he was, indeed, her soulmate.

She found herself smiling back at him. 'Mattie's going to love that,' she said softly. 'So will I.'

Josh looked so relieved. 'It's what friends do,' he said.

Stevie took a deep breath and her smile widened, although the edges of it might have wobbled a little. 'Let's get this paperwork sorted,' she said. 'Friends get to celebrate stuff like this, too, don't they?'

CHAPTER SEVEN

GLOUCESTER GENERAL HOSPITAL'S rooftop vegetable garden had become 'their' spot.

A relatively private space. Sometimes the
only space they could find time to snatch
a moment of being close enough to touch
when it had been too long since they'd been
together away from work. Not that they did
touch, of course—with anything more than
perhaps some eye contact that went on a little too long—because the knowledge of any
extra dimension to the friendship was also
something that belonged only to them. A secret that nobody else needed to know and one
that added a rather delicious frisson to their
professional relationship.

If Ruby's bunions didn't make it prefera-
ble for her to put her feet up in the staffroom
during her breaks, rather than climbing all
those stairs and then trying to find some-

where at least a bit sheltered from a potentially chilly breeze, she might have guessed there was something more going on between Josh and Stevie but, then, it didn't happen often enough to have even caught the attention of the volunteers who cared for the gardens or any other staff members who ventured up here.

And if anyone had walked close enough to hear what they were saying, they would most likely have only heard a professional kind of discussion happening between the head of the paediatric department and that nurse with the amazing hair.

Like the one they were having at the moment.

'I feel so sorry for Toby's mum, Julia.' Stevie took a sip of the takeaway coffee she'd purchased, along with some sandwiches, in the staff cafeteria. 'Mattie used to climb on everything when he was a toddler. He could have easily fallen off the couch and broken his collarbone like Toby did.'

'Common injury,' Josh agreed. 'And, most of the time, it heals up without any complications.'

'But Toby's been left with an arm that barely functions, even after all that physiotherapy. He can't bend his elbow or flex his fingers or even hang on to a toy.'

'Brachial plexus injuries can be very damaging.'

'It's quite a common birth injury, isn't it? The nerve roots that go from the spinal cord to the arm and hand are between C5 and T1 so they get stretched and damaged if the head and shoulder get too far apart?'

Josh nodded. 'Regeneration of axons can be amazing in babies, though, so it pays to wait and track progress before doing anything invasive like a nerve graft or transfer.'

'What's the difference?' Stevie loved that she could ask any question of Josh and never feel like it was stupid. She was loving learning from him, as well. Partly because it meant they were never, ever going to run out of interesting things to talk about but also because it gave her glimpses of an exciting future where she might be able to specialise in a new area of paediatric nursing.

'A nerve graft takes a section of nerve from somewhere else in the body, usually the leg, and it's used to replace the damaged nerve. A nerve transfer, which is what Toby's going to have, is a newer technique that can have a brilliant result. Instead of grafting in a section of another nerve, they redirect a nearby nerve so that it targets the muscles that can't function. There's a learning curve to getting the nerve to work properly but the end results can be outstanding.' Josh was smiling. 'Microsurgery is fascinating. I'm hoping I can go and watch the surgery.'

He was holding her gaze as well and Stevie knew he understood exactly how fascinated she also was.

'Maybe I could arrange for you to come and watch it too. It'll have to be in a theatre with a gallery given that there'll be a lot of people who want to be there.'

'Oh…do you think I'd be allowed?'

'Let me see what I can do.'

He was still smiling. Still holding her gaze but, suddenly, this was anything but professional. That attraction could spark between them like a lightning bolt and…well…it simply wasn't appropriate. Hospitals might be well known for passionate liaisons between staff members but very few would ever shut themselves into a linen cupboard—or even snatch a kiss in a rooftop garden.

It was Stevie who sucked in a deep breath and broke that eye contact. 'So who's going to do the surgery? Julia sounded quite confused after that family meeting this morning. I think she was really intimidated by how many doctors were there.'

'Mmm...' Josh's smile had been amused as Stevie had taken charge of ending that meaningful moment between them. Now it twisted into something more like a frown. 'I'll go and have another chat with her before Toby goes home today. There were a lot of people in the meeting room. We had a consultant radiologist to go through the results of the MRI. Then there was the orthopaedic surgeon who looked after Toby when he was admitted with his fractured clavicle and the neurosurgeon that Toby got referred to.'

'But he's not doing the operation? Julia said something about it apparently being really lucky that some visiting expert was going to be available.'

Josh nodded again. 'Yeah. Some hot-shot paediatric plastic surgeon who did his advanced training in the States and is getting recognised as a leader in the field.'

'A *plastic* surgeon?'

Josh laughed. 'They do a lot more than superficial stuff. Rehabilitation plastic surgery is about function more than appearance. This guy—Lachlan McKendry, his name is—is getting well known for his success in micro-surgery techniques.'

'And he's coming to work here?'

'Not exactly. He got headhunted from the States to join a private clinic in London, from what I've been told. He's got family here or something. Anyway, he also agreed to do a series of lectures and some advanced training in hospitals not too far from London and the Gloucester area got chosen first. So I guess Toby *is* really lucky. Our neurosurgeon, David, is excited about working with this guy.'

'And Julia thought the surgery might be as early as next week?'

'We're having another meeting later this afternoon when Mr McKendry will be here to get briefed. He may well want more detailed tests to happen first, like a CT myelography scan that uses a contrast to give a very detailed picture of the spinal cord and nerve roots.'

'He'll need sedation for that, too, I guess. Like he had for the MRI today?'

'Yes.' Josh checked his watch. 'I'd better go and see Julia. I'm sure Toby's awake enough to be discharged now.' He scrunched up the paper bag that had held his sandwiches and gestured towards Stevie's bag. 'You all done?'

'Yep. It wasn't the world's best sandwich.'

'Nothing's as good as your mousetraps for lunch.'

'I'll make some more.' Stevie got to her feet and brushed crumbs off her coat. 'I could send some with Mattie on Thursday for when you do your Big Brother thing.'

'Fabulous.' Josh was leading the way through the raised garden beds towards the door that led to the stairwell. 'Did he tell you where we're going this week?'

'No. I got the impression it was boy stuff that I didn't need to know about.'

Josh laughed. 'He's right. We're going to a hardware store to check out tools we're going to need. We might do a bit of internet surfing to find some instructional videos as well.'

'Boy stuff, huh?' Stevie had to pass close to Josh as he held the door open for her and she deliberately paused for just a heartbeat at a point where she was close enough to feel his body heat because it was too delicious to resist. And maybe she was having another one of those glimpses into a future that could hold something even more exciting than advanced qualifications in a nursing specialty. Even better than owning her own home and achieving an independence she'd dreamed of. She could almost hear an echo of Josh's voice in that glimpse as well, saying that teaching Mattie about renovation and tools would keep them busy for ever.

Don't go there...

The warning was hardwired into the same part of her brain. She knew better than to buy into the kind of dream that could set you up for a broken heart. Yes, it was there but she wasn't going to trust it.

Not yet...

And it was easy to diffuse. To turn it into something very different. Stevie flicked her gaze up to graze his. 'I'll have you know,' she said softly, 'that DIY is one of my many, many talents.'

She loved the way she could trust that Josh would always respond to her like this. That the level of attraction was always so easily— and equally—ignited. She saw the way the muscles in his neck moved as he swallowed. The way his eyes darkened to almost black as they locked onto hers. From behind her, as she moved past, she could hear the way he needed to clear his throat.

'He's pretty excited, isn't he? About the move?'

'Counting sleeps,' Stevie agreed.

'So am I,' Josh murmured as he caught up with her at the first landing, his hand brushing hers on the railing of the stairs. 'We're almost going to be neighbours.'

'Colleagues, friends *and* neighbours…' Stevie threw a smile over her shoulder as she sped up her descent to the next landing. She was laughing as her mouth ran away with the words that were coming from nowhere, perhaps fuelled by the heat that simply the brush of his hand had generated. 'What more could you possibly want?'

With the door swinging open and a lab technician carrying a coolbox coming into the stairwell, there was no chance of hearing any response Josh might have made to that impulsive question. Which was probably just as well, Stevie decided later that afternoon as she hurried away from work at the end of her shift. Josh's aversion to anything like permanence, or family, was just as hardwired into his brain as her own difficulty in trusting men had been.

Had he even answered her? Maybe he

might have thought she was pushing boundaries that he'd made very clear a long time ago. It wasn't as if she'd seen him on the ward again this afternoon and had had the opportunity to share a glance or a smile and reassure herself that nothing had changed.

Stevie had walked to work that morning but the quickest route home was to cut diagonally through the car park to get to the main road. And maybe it was because she was thinking about Josh that made it so easy to spot him even well up ahead, walking across her intended path towards the main hospital building.

'Hi,' she called. 'What are you doing out here?'

He didn't seem to have heard her. Or was he ignoring her? Stevie's smile faltered. It looked as if he was just going to keep going, cross her path and not even look at her. He was looking over his shoulder, in fact, his attention seemingly caught by an extremely flash car. A silver car, which rang a vague bell for Stevie but she ignored it because she was more worried than ever that she might have been skating on thin ice by putting labels on their relationship when it was something they never really talked about.

What was worse was that, when Josh did turn his head, he seemed to look straight at Stevie and not even blink as he focused on the hospital buildings ahead of him. As if he didn't see her. Or didn't want to? What on earth was going on? And what was he doing, wearing a suit? Josh never wore suits. He often came to work in jeans before he changed into his scrubs.

'Hey… *Josh?*'

She knew he had to be able to hear her but he was still walking away. Stevie had the sudden, horrible realisation of what it might be like if whatever it was they had between them at the moment fizzled out and she was aware of a beat of fear. But, at the same time, the Josh she knew would never treat anybody this rudely. Bewilderment coated the fear and somehow became anger.

'Oi!' she shouted. 'What's going on, Josh? Are you seriously just going to walk away from me?'

That stopped him in his tracks. He turned to face Stevie as she kept marching towards him. But then her steps faltered and it felt as if the earth's axis was tipping slightly off kilter—but not in a good way, like it had the first time Josh had kissed her.

He looked weird. And kind of angry.

'What is it with people calling me *Josh*?' he demanded. 'It seems to happen everywhere I go around here. And who the hell are *you*?'

Stevie opened her mouth and then closed it again, her brain spinning as she took in the fact that this *wasn't* Josh. It was someone who looked astonishingly like him, however, but up close she could see the differences. This man was a little more solid, perhaps— his hair was shorter and he had some carefully managed designer stubble going on. Most of all, the way he was looking at her held nothing of the warmth she was so used to seeing in Josh's eyes now.

And that was when something clicked. Stevie could hear again a snatch of a conversation she'd overheard in the staffroom a few weeks ago between Ruby and Josh.

'*Saw you over at Cheltenham Central Hospital...*

'*That's a flash new car you've got... Silvery thing...*'

'*Good to see that you've had a shave since then, anyway...*'

Stevie opened her mouth again. And swallowed hard.

'My name's Stevie,' she told him. 'And I'm sorry I shouted at you like that but...but you look incredibly like a friend of mine. Someone who works here. I...thought he was ignoring me.'

'Ah...' His smile was polite. 'And this friend is called Josh, I take it?'

'Yes...'

'I'm Lachlan,' he told her. 'Lachlan McKendry. If you work here, perhaps you can help? I'm heading for a meeting in the paediatric department.'

'Oh...of course. I've heard about you. You're the famous plastic surgeon.'

The way his eyebrow quirked stole Stevie's breath away. He was *so* like Josh it was spooky. They said everybody had a doppelganger out there somewhere but this was impossible.

Unless...

Stevie knew that her intense stare was coming across as being rude. That this renowned paediatric surgeon had probably decided it would be better to go and find the department he was looking for by himself. Yes...he was turning on his heel as if he couldn't wait to get away from her.

'Wait...' Stevie sucked in a quick breath.

'I know this might sound totally crazy but…
are you, by any chance, adopted?'

That stopped him for a second time. His
expression was more dumbfounded than
angry now.

'Not that it's any of your business,' he said
slowly. 'But, no, I'm not.'

'Sorry…' Stevie bit her lip. 'It's just that
you look so much like Josh, you could be
brothers. Twins, even.'

That made him laugh but then he shook his
head. 'Sounds like the stuff of fairy tales. If
you'll excuse me, I don't want to be late for
my meeting.'

His meeting.

With Josh and the other specialists involved in Toby's case, like the neurosurgeon,
David and the orthopaedic surgeon and all
their respective registrars.

Stevie could imagine how shocking it
would be to come face to face with someone who looked so much like herself that it
would be like looking into a slightly cracked
mirror and it certainly wouldn't be something she wanted to happen in front of other
people. And, even if her wild idea that these
men could be closely related was no more
than the remotest possibility, it was still a

diatric department so it's who you've come here to see, anyway, but…' Stevie's brief head shake acknowledged that this was too complicated to try and explain. 'I'll be back in a few minutes and then you'll understand why this is so important.'

It wasn't simply that she had run down the stairs so fast that had Stevie's heart thumping hard as she tapped on Josh's office door a minute or two later.

'Josh?'

The note of urgency in her voice made him look up instantly but Stevie couldn't offer any kind of reassurance, like a smile. What was happening here wasn't just some strange coincidence. Stevie just knew it was huge and she knew that Josh could see that in her face because he was already getting to his feet and his forehead was creased with concern.

'What's wrong, Stevie?'

'Come with me. There's something you need to see.'

'I know.' Stevie had her hands on the heavy door, ready to push it open, but she paused to catch his gaze. 'Whatever this is,' she said quietly, 'it's going to be okay…'

There was something in the depths of those gloriously hazel eyes that Josh had never seen before. It felt like a promise— that she would do whatever it took to *make* it okay?

No wonder Josh felt like he might be stepping far too close to the edge of a cliff as he followed her outside. And then he found himself staring at the man who was clearly waiting for them and he could actually *feel* his world being turned inside out.

'Josh? This is Lachlan McKendry. Lachlan, this is Josh Stanmore. Um… I thought it might be a good idea if you two had a bit of time before your meeting.'

Neither Josh nor Lachlan responded. They were both staring at each other.

Fascinated.

Spooked.

Josh could feel Stevie watching him. He could hear the concern in her voice in the way it faltered. 'Do you want me to stay?'

He turned towards her and, for a moment in this free-fall of what felt like a seis-

mic change in his life, Josh knew that his
friendship with Stevie was a safe haven if
he needed one. Not that he could run away
from this. And it was not something that anyone other than himself and the man in front
of him could deal with, but knowing that he
had someone he could trust who was in his
corner was enough to give him the strength
he needed.

He gave his head only a single shake.
'Thanks, Stevie.' He held her gaze long
enough to let her know just how much he
appreciated the fact that she'd given him a
chance to deal with this privately, at least to
begin with. Had she chosen this obscure part
of Gloucester General because she'd remembered that it was where he'd brought her to
protect her own privacy? It felt like a lifetime ago but it was a reminder of how solid
their friendship had become. How much trust
there was between them.

'We'll talk soon,' he promised.

'Soon' turned out to be three days later,
thanks to a day off for Stevie, a shift that
didn't coincide and the understandable con-
fusion laced with astonishment that meant
Josh needed to spend any free time he had

right now with Lachlan McKendry. Apart from a text message or two that assured Stevie he was fine and a promise that he wasn't going to let anything interfere with his time with Mattie, she had no idea how Josh was really coping until he dropped Mattie home after their Big Brother session on Thursday. Stevie knew then that she had been right to feel worried.

Josh looked as if he hadn't slept properly for days. As if he'd lost weight, too, and he even had a noticeable five o'clock shadow today, which made him look even more like Stevie remembered Lachlan had looked. The almost haunted look in Josh's eyes squeezed her heart so hard that it hurt and he was holding her gaze with an intensity that suggested he had been missing her company as much as she had been missing his.

'When did you last have a proper meal?' she asked.

'I'm not that hungry, to be honest.'

Stevie thought quickly. She already had Mattie's favourite fish fingers and chips dinner keeping warm in the oven but she could hardly offer some of that to Josh. He clearly needed to eat something, though. And maybe he needed someone to talk to even more. He

was still holding her gaze and, if they hadn't been able to hear Mattie in the background, she was quite sure he would be kissing her senseless. The desire for that to *be* happening was so strong that Stevie knew she had to, at least, have some time with Josh.

'There's an Italian restaurant down the road,' she told him. 'Cheap and cheerful but they do the best lasagne I've ever tasted and their fresh salad and garlic bread is to die for.' Yeah…he was hungry. Stevie could see the spark of interest in those dark eyes. 'How 'bout I meet you there in ten minutes? I just need to get my neighbour to keep an eye on Mattie. Someone has to make sure you have a decent meal. You're not on call tonight, are you?'

'No.' Josh was smiling now. Maybe he liked that she was taking charge and trying to look after him?

'Have a glass of wine while you're waiting, then.'

Stevie put her hand on his arm to encourage him to turn and, despite her body's protest that what she wanted to do more than anything was to pull him back and into her arms, she gave him a gentle shove on his back to make sure she didn't give in to that

desire. And to make sure Josh didn't hang around to protest that he wasn't hungry.

'I'll see you there,' she said, closing the door behind him.

The carafe of red wine looked to be half-empty by the time Stevie arrived at the small, local restaurant and the plate of pizza-style garlic bread only had crumbs left on the red, gingham napkin that matched the tablecloth.

'I was hungrier than I thought I was,' Josh admitted. 'Shall I order some more?'

Stevie nodded as he signalled the waiter. 'I'll have a glass of wine, too, please. And then I want to know what's going on.'

Josh shook his head as he poured her some wine from the carafe. 'I don't even know where to begin. It's crazy...'

'Start at the beginning. From when I left you on the roof. I haven't even *seen* you since then.' Stevie added a smile to counteract what could have been interpreted as a somewhat desperate undertone to her words. She couldn't let Josh know just how much she'd been missing him. That she might be starting to depend on his presence in her life?

Josh was smiling back. 'I'm sorry. And you're the only person I can really talk to

about this—the only one who will get just how much of a shock it is.'

'So you *are* brothers?' Stevie tucked away those words of being the only person he could talk to about this. She knew they would feel like a verbal hug when she pulled them out again, later.

'The first thing I asked him was where and when he was born. Same place as me—in Cheltenham. Same year as me. Same day...'

'Oh, my God,' Stevie whispered. 'I knew it. You're *twins*...'

'Lachlan was as shocked as I was. He couldn't believe that his mother could have given one of her babies away. He decided that maybe I'd been stolen. That his mother had been told one of her twins had died or something to cover it up.' Josh stopped and took a deep breath. 'But the whole time we were talking about it we were watching each other, you know? And it was so weird. His voice is so like mine and we'd start speaking at the same time and we'd move at the same time and...it was like looking in a mirror.'

'Did you go to that meeting?'

'No. We had to postpone it. It's not as if the surgery is urgent and neither of us would have been able to focus, which would have

could become one day. This was flesh and blood kind of family. Someone that you had a genetic bond with. Someone who could drag a painful past that Josh had kept secret into a present that he couldn't escape.

This could turn his world upside down.

There would be time later to worry about how this might affect her and, more importantly, how it might affect Mattie, but right now she had to try and engineer a way that could provide the privacy she knew was essential for two men who could both be about to face something life-changing. It was only when Stevie noticed she had gone above the level for the paediatric department that she realised her subconscious had come up with the perfect plan. She pushed open the heavy doors that led out to the rooftop garden where she'd been, only hours ago, with Josh.

'What's going on?' Lachlan blinked as he looked around.

'Wait here.' Stevie injected the same kind of authority into her voice that she'd used with Mattie when he'd been too little to understand why he couldn't just run out onto a pedestrian crossing. 'Trust me, please… There's someone you have to meet before you do anything else. He's the head of the pae-

potential bomb that was about to be thrown into Josh's life.

The urge to protect him was as fierce as any Stevie had ever felt to protect Mattie. The kind of urge that could only be this strong when you loved someone enough for their welfare to be more important than your own. Not that Stevie was going to take any time to think about what was going on in her head—or her heart—and what it might mean for the future. She just knew that she wasn't about to let Josh face this without her being there to support him if he needed her.

'I know exactly where you need to be,' she told Lachlan McKendry. 'Follow me.'

They walked in silence as Stevie led Lachlan swiftly into Gloucester General Hospital, along corridors and up the stairs. She couldn't make small talk because there was too much going on in her head.

What if the almost impossible was somehow true? That Josh was about to discover he had a cousin, perhaps? Or a brother? It would force something on him that he believed he had never needed and had no desire for now.

Family.

Real family. Not a chosen sort of family that she might dream that she and Mattie

made it a waste of time for everybody involved. Plus, I'm not ready for the grapevine to get hold of this information with all the gossip that'll happen. I don't think anybody saw us together but thank goodness you intercepted him before he turned up at the paediatric ward. Can you imagine how Ruby would have reacted?'

The fragrant, steamy triangles of fresh garlic bread straight from the pizza oven were placed in front of them, along with a big bowl of fresh salad and the lasagne they'd both ordered.

'She would have whisked him off to her office and interrogated him,' Stevie joked. 'Nicely but, oh, so thoroughly.'

'Exactly. So thank you for giving us the best private space we could have had—until Lachlan came to my place the next evening, that is, and, man, did we need the private space then.'

'Why?'

'He was wrecked.' Josh was silent for a moment as he tasted his food. 'Oh, boy...this is good.' He ate in silence for another minute but then put his fork down. 'This is a hell of a lot harder for him than it is for me, I think. He didn't even know he was adopted.'

Stevie nodded as she added a scoop of salad onto her plate. 'He sounded quite sure he *wasn't*, when I suggested it.'

'He went home after we met and accused his mother of giving away his twin brother and demanded to know why. It sounds like it ended up being the most enormous row. She said she had no idea he was one of twins but, even if she'd known, she wouldn't have wanted two babies. She didn't even want one and she'd only agreed to the adoption to save her marriage. Lachlan said it made sense of a lot of stuff but it still did his head in. I think he found it a bit cathartic to talk about it, to be honest. We were up pretty much all night and there might have been a bit of whisky involved.'

Stevie blinked as Josh paused to eat a few more mouthfuls. The chance meeting between twin brothers who'd been separated as babies was astonishing enough. That they'd both had less than loving upbringings was not so much of a coincidence as a tragedy but it sounded as if a bonding process was well underway.

'She lives locally,' Josh added. 'The mother. Jocelyn or Josephine? I can't remember. Anyway, she's not actually that far

from me. In one of those estates I was telling you about—with a huge mansion and its own forest? The McKendrys have family money from way back, which was why Lachlan's father was desperate for an heir, I guess, but he was also a cardiothoracic surgeon in some exclusive private hospital in London—famous enough to have been given a knighthood. Lachlan said there was never any choice about the career he was going to have, right from when he got sent off to boarding school when he was only about six years old.'

Stevie shook her head. 'Unbelievable.'

'He kind of rebelled, by going into plastic surgery instead of cardiac or neurosurgery. And then he took off as soon as he could to do postgrad training and work in the States.'

'What's brought him back here?'

'He'd been headhunted by a children's hospital in London and came back last year because he said he was, finally, a bit homesick. He's been in demand for lecture tours and specialist training and so on since he got back but the Gloucester area is the first one he accepted and that was because he can still travel to London if he needs to and he's got some major family stuff he needs to sort out.'

'I guess his parents are getting older?'

'His father died more than a decade ago. It's his mother who's causing the problems and she sounds like a very difficult woman.'

'She sounds horrible. How could you adopt a baby like it was some kind of sticking plaster to hold a marriage together?'

Josh shrugged and his expression reminded Stevie of why he'd turned his back on the concept of marriage and family long ago. That those kinds of relationships couldn't be trusted. That they could do more harm than good, even.

'Seems like her carers don't like her much, either. They keep resigning.'

'She needs carers?'

'Full time.' Josh nodded. 'With medical training. I think he said she's got brittle diabetes. Or asthma. Maybe both—I've forgotten everything we said. It wasn't just Lachlan spilling an outline of his entire history—I was doing the same. It was like we had to catch up with as much as possible, as soon as possible.'

He reached for his wine glass and took a long sip, his gaze holding Stevie's over the rim.

'You're the only person I've ever said any-

CHAPTER EIGHT

JOSH KNEW WHERE they were going as soon as they started heading upstairs and the fact that Stevie wanted them to be somewhere as private as possible was alarming, to say the least.

Had something happened to Mattie?

But Stevie's son seemed to be the last thing on her mind right then.

'Do you remember that day when Ruby thought you had a new car?' Stevie was racing up the stairs. 'A really flash one?'

'Yeah…something ridiculous like a Maserati.'

'And she said you'd needed a shave?' Stevie was out of breath as she reached the door at the top of the stairwell and she paused to look back at Josh. 'She was telling the truth.'

'What? I have no idea what you're talking about.'

thing to about my background but… I don't know, it just felt so easy to talk to Lachlan. We'd only just met but I felt like I'd known him for ever.'

'You kind of have,' Stevie said softly. 'You shared a womb for nine months.'

But Josh shook his head. 'I don't think I buy into that "twin" stuff. Or even an automatic genetic connection.' He shook his head again, as if he didn't want to even think about it, turning his attention to his meal again.

'Anyway,' he said a minute or two later, 'Mrs McKendry's housekeeper threatened to walk out recently so Lachlan decided to kill two birds with one stone. He's basing himself at the family mansion while he divides his time between hospitals here and his work in London and he's planning to use the three-month stint to get some kind of permanent arrangement in place for his mother. Or his "ex" mother, as he was calling her by the time we talked.'

'So he's here for a while longer, then?'

'Yes. Another couple of months, at least. I think that day that Ruby clocked him was his first day at Cheltenham Central. He's going to start with us next week, to line up Toby's surgery and some lectures and demonstrations he's going to present on new suture techniques amongst other stuff. What gets done in Emergency or even elective surgery can have major repercussions down the track for anyone, but especially for paediatrics. I'm looking forward to learning the latest myself.'

Stevie ate the last forkful of her salad. 'No wonder you were both up all night. Sounds like you talked about everything.'

Josh nodded slowly. 'Seemed like that at the time. Now it feels like we've barely started.'

'I'd like to meet him again.'

Stevie tried not to advertise just how intrigued she was to discover more. And to see what changes it might mean for Josh's view of the world—and family?

Oh, no…she couldn't go there. Poor Josh had quite enough to deal with, without adding any hint of pressure from her for something that wasn't even on an agenda. She offered him a smile. 'I mean, if he's your twin I'm sure he's a nice guy.'

To her relief, Josh smiled back. He had a bit more colour in his cheeks as well so maybe he was feeling better after eating.

'I told him about you,' he said. 'After he

asked if I'd ever been married. Or if I have a girlfriend.'

'Oh?' Stevie's heart skipped a beat. Had their friendship been promoted to the status of a relationship? She caught her bottom lip between her teeth at the same moment her breath caught in her chest. The longing to hear Josh say that he considered her to be his girlfriend was powerful enough to over-ride anything else.

But Josh's smile was fading. 'Turns out we both have the same aversion to permanence in that department,' he said. 'Weird, huh?'

One side of Stevie's mouth quirked into a wry smile but she had no words to find. The stab of something a lot deeper than dis-appointment was definitely sharp enough to remind her of what heartbreak was like. Enough to make it very clear that she had let herself get into a dangerous place where she could end up getting badly hurt. Was that why it was called 'falling' in love?

'So, what do you think?'

'Sorry, what?' Stevie had been so lost in her own thoughts she'd missed what Josh had been saying as he pushed his empty plate away.

'I was saying that Lachlan suggested a

night out. Apparently there's a locum nurse who's living in and looking after his mother and Lachlan would like to take her out to a nice restaurant somewhere to give her an evening off. He wants us to come as well. I think he's as glad as I am that we didn't have to come face to face with each other for the first time in front of other people so he'd like to thank you properly.'

Josh was reaching across the table as he spoke to cover Stevie's hand with his own and she could feel the warmth of that touch spread from her fingers to her arm and then wash into every cell in her body to pool, deep in her belly.

'Sounds fun.' Somehow she managed to keep her tone light. 'Let me know when so I can sort a babysitter.'

'Next week, maybe? Or the week after that? We need to get Toby's surgery out of the way first, I think, but it would be better if it was before your settlement on the cottage, wouldn't it? You'll be busy getting things sorted and then moving and I guess it might be harder to find a babysitter until you know people in the village.'

Life was certainly about to change in the near future but Stevie's excitement about the move was suddenly tinged with apprehension about other changes that might be coming—for both herself and Josh. That stab of more than disappointment was still there, deepening into a kind of chill that was more than enough to smother that delicious heat. It felt cold enough to be something very like fear. She couldn't leave Mattie out of the equation, either. Josh might have promised never to hurt her son but who knew what was going to happen in the future, when such major changes had been triggered in Josh's own life?

'Speaking of babysitting...' Stevie scrunched up her napkin as she got to her feet. 'I'd better get back and let Mrs Johnston get home.'

It took another couple of weeks before Lachlan McKendry was ready to do the nerve transfer surgery that would hopefully restore shoulder and arm function to two-year-old Toby. More tests had been necessary, including a repeat electrical study of nerve function right before the surgery was scheduled.

The gallery of the operating theatre was full but nobody had queried why Josh had someone from the paediatric nursing staff sitting right beside him in the front row. Perhaps because it was now common knowledge that it was Josh's brother who was the star performer in this intricate surgery?

There were screens that allowed them a close-up look at what was happening below and Josh had been watching in fascination from when the first felt pen marks had been made on the child's back to mark anatomical points for the meticulous dissection Lachlan was making to expose the nerves he was targeting.

'So, we're going to use distal branches of the spinal accessory nerve to neurotise the suprascapular nerve, which is the classic approach to repairing a damaged brachial plexus network. I'm working slowly here, because there are a lot of small vessels and I don't want to have to cauterise them when I'm this close to the nerve. I hope none of you are expecting an early lunch today.'

The ripple of sound was too muted to be labelled as laughter. It was more like an acknowledgement that what they were witnessing was of far more interest than lunch but it did make Josh glance sideways, because anytime he thought about lunch there was always a background thought of mousetraps. And of Stevie.

As if she could feel the touch of his gaze,

she shifted her head so that she could glance at Josh for a moment, instead of the screen. There was a hint of a smile tugging at one corner of her mouth and her eyes were glowing. She was loving this opportunity to get so close to the action that she turned back to watch again almost instantly but Josh let his gaze linger on her profile for a heartbeat longer.

He'd been right in thinking that Stevie was his safe haven. If anything, over the last few weeks she'd become such a rock he couldn't imagine not having her in his life. So many things had changed and what had helped him more than anything in coping with it all was talking to Stevie about it. He'd told her things he would never dream about saying to anyone else and her responses often made him feel not only understood but could give him a new perspective. Like that late-night phone conversation last week…

'I felt kind of jealous for a while, you know? Lachlan had everything money could buy. He never had to take a job in a bar or delivering pizzas to get through med school. He had a home where he was wanted. A father who was proud of every prize he got at school.'

'But was he any happier than you were, do you think?'

'No. I don't think he was...'

Lachlan was certainly in his element right now. His voice was calm and confident as he kept up a commentary for his audience.

'I'm going for the donor nerve first, because finding the suprascapular notch and nerve is a bit more challenging.' There was almost a smile to be heard in his voice now. 'But success is always sweeter after a challenge, isn't it?'

It wasn't the first time that Lachlan turned his head, signalling that he needed perspiration swabbed from his forehead and it made Josh frown. Was Lachlan under more stress than it seemed? Could the challenges that had intruded on his personal life be having a background effect on his professional performance?

At least they were working towards getting used to the bombshell of discovering each other. Getting to know each other. And having the news hit the hospital grapevine hadn't been nearly as confronting as Josh had feared, because—apart from Stevie—nobody knew he was adopted and nobody could guess that he hadn't even known himself that he had a brother. People assumed he'd just kept his personal life private and they respected that. So far, nobody had even tried to find out why they had different surnames. Perhaps they were still too intrigued by the similarities between Josh and Lachlan to move on to what was different.

'Here we go…' Lachlan's voice was clear and confident. 'I'm opening up the trapezius muscle now. You'd expect the nerve to be in the muscle but it isn't. It's below the muscle, in the fatty layer. Again, I'm going slowly.'

He was being so careful—the way Josh was with any procedure he performed. There was no denying how similar he and Lachlan were. It seemed like every time they were together they discovered something else they shared, like a favourite colour or food or movie. And, sometimes, it was something on a physical level, like a gesture. Or the fact they both had the same, slightly crooked eye tooth. Things were adding up, that's for sure, and Josh was beginning to wonder if Stevie was right about a genetic connection. A 'twin' thing? She'd said something else about it the other day.

You have family, Josh. It's not a matter of choice. This is real. Genetic. You have more in common with each other than you'll ever have with anyone else on earth. A bond that's there whether you want it or not. And it can be a bond that's more important than anything else—like the one I have with Mattie.'

But Stevie had built that bond from the moment she'd chosen to go through with her pregnancy and it had been strengthened every day since. Josh had no history with his brother at all. Could that bond still be significant? The idea of whether nature or nurture was dominant in shaping personalities and lives was a topic that had just become very personal for Josh but there was no denying they both shared the same passion for medicine.

Even as his thoughts strayed on one level, Josh was focused on the screen, watching every tiny, careful snip Lachlan was making to get through the muscle to find the nerve he needed.

'Some of you might be interested in reading about new advances in nerve and tendon transfers.' Lachlan seemed to have the same ability to be thinking on different levels because his hands never faltered in their task. 'It's an exciting field that's offering a lot of promise in restoring function for people with tetraplegia, for example. Giving them enough movement to be able to gain independence in feeding themselves, or driving a car. Ah... there we go. There's the suprascapular nerve. Can I have a vessel loop, please?'

Josh watched as the nerve was identified by the soft loop and then cut to leave the end ready to be joined to the functioning nerve. Yes...he did have a lot in common with Lachlan but their connection had reached a totally new level just last night when they'd stayed late at the hospital as Lachlan had explained the detail of today's surgery to Josh. As they'd stood outside, ready to go in their separate directions, Lachlan had paused.

'Do you think it made it easier, knowing all along that you'd been adopted?'

'I think it made it worse. I knew I was different. That I didn't belong, somehow, but I didn't know why until a "real" son came along and I wasn't wanted any more.'

But Lachlan had shaken his head. *'I never knew and I think that was worse because I didn't belong either but I never knew why. Until I met you.'*

Maybe it had been at that moment that Josh had begun to change his mind about the existence of a meaningful genetic connection between people. Something that would never change. That could be trusted, no matter what.

And, if he'd been wrong about that, maybe there were other assumptions about relationships he needed to revisit.

As he watched his brother perform the extraordinary task of joining tiny nerves together with sutures that were almost invisible to the naked eye, Josh felt himself letting go of some nameless tension. Even his body relaxed, to the point where he could feel his thigh touching Stevie's leg.

Could she feel that heat? It was burning through layers of fabric for Josh.

What would she say if she knew that his focus wasn't completely on the end of Toby's surgery now, he wondered, as his gaze drifted from the screen to Stevie's profile again. What if she knew he was thinking that she might need to revisit some of her own assumptions—like the one about genetic connections being 'real' because you had no choice about them?

Surely a chosen connection could be just as real? Like the one that had grown so strong between him and Stevie? It was more than he'd ever found with any other woman on earth.

Again, it seemed that Stevie could feel his gaze, in the same way he was so aware of the subtle touching of their legs. She barely moved her head but her gaze managed to find his. And hold it. And it seemed as though she was answering a question that he hadn't re-alised was showing in his eyes.

Telling him that she agreed with him about the connection they'd found.

Promising him that it could be trusted…

CHAPTER NINE

DESPITE BEING DETERMINED not to build any hopes high enough to mean her heart would shatter into many more pieces when things changed, it was impossible to ignore the significance of being invited out to dinner with Josh and his twin brother. By the time a date had been agreed on—at rather short notice, in the end—and a restaurant booked, the event suddenly took on an importance that was generating rather a lot of tension.

It felt like a *date*…

As if Josh was happy to go out in public with her as his partner. To introduce her properly to the only real family he had. To potentially be seen, in fact, by people who worked in at Gloucester General, in which case the grapevine would have a new rumour to disperse and embellish.

Stevie could have been distinctly apprehensive by the potential step forward this outing could represent in her relationship with Josh but she wasn't allowing herself to think about that. Living in the moment had worked very well when she'd decided she might as well make the most of one night with Josh Stanmore so that's what she was doing again. Making the most of what could be a fantasy date.

When she heard that Lachlan had chosen one of the most prestigious restaurants in the region, her first reaction—apart from the nervousness that came from knowing that she was going to feel like a fish out of water—was to thank her lucky stars that she already had a suitable dress.

Nobody needed to know that it had been a fabulous find in a London charity shop a couple of years ago. A dress so gorgeous that Stevie had had to try it on, even though she'd known how unlikely it was that she would ever have an occasion that she would be able to wear it. And trying it on had been a mistake because there was no way she could leave it behind in the shop. Not when she'd discovered that such a rich shade of burgundy could look so amazing with the deep, auburn colour of her hair. Or that the combination of the cross-over bodice that exposed just enough of her shoulders, and the hem of the full skirt being so much higher at front than the back to reveal glimpses of her legs as she moved, made it the sexiest dress she'd ever tried on.

So she'd bought the dress and it had hung at the back of her wardrobe ever since. Sometimes, Stevie would notice it and stop a moment to touch it, loving the feel of the lace fabric and remembering how the silk lining had slipped over her skin like a lover's touch. That feeling was still there as she put it on to actually wear out for the very first time, along with relief that it was still a perfect fit, but there was something a lot more intense that *had* changed. That slip of silk against her skin didn't give her a fantasy moment of some imaginary lover. This time, it made her think only of Josh and how his touch made her feel.

How she knew, right down to her bones, that she would never find another lover who could make her feel like that.

Another man that she could trust enough to love as much as she loved Josh Stanmore.

Mattie's jaw dropped when he saw her come out of the bathroom when she'd finished getting into her dress and doing her hair and make-up.

'You look beautiful, Mum… Like a princess.'

'Thanks, hon.'

'Are you really going out to dinner with Josh?'

'I am.'

'Because you're his girlfriend?'

Oh…help… There was no mistaking that gleam of hope in her son's dark eyes. He really wanted her and Josh to be together, didn't he? For Josh to be part of his future as a lot more than a Big Brother mentor, and that sounded a note of alarm that Stevie knew she'd have to deal with properly at some point. But not right now because that could spoil this fantasy and the temptation to indulge in the pleasure of living the dream for just a few hours was too strong. It wasn't going to hurt anyone, especially Mattie, because she wouldn't let that happen.

Stevie found a smile that she hoped was both reassuring but casual enough that it would help let him down gently when that time came. 'Because I'm his friend,' she said. 'And I met his brother a little while ago. He's coming too, so it's not like a date or anything.'

'Josh has got a brother?' Mattie's eyes widened as he was completely distracted. 'I never knew that.'

'Josh didn't either.' Stevie bent to drop a kiss on Mattie's head. 'But it's a long story and it'll have to wait until you see Josh again because it's his story to tell, not mine. Now… I'm going to go and tell Mrs Johnson I'm ready to go. Are you all set for tonight?'

'Yeah… I'm going to talk to Gran and do some more packing. Are we really moving next week?'

'We are.'

'And Lucky's going to come and live with us straight away?'

'That's something else to talk about with Josh. He might want us to be properly settled in before Lucky comes.'

'Talk about it tonight,' Mattie instructed. 'Tell him I want Lucky to come on the first day we move in. I want him to sleep on the end of my bed.'

The scruffy little dog was the last thing on Stevie's mind, however, when she found herself sitting in Josh's car a short time later and they were on their way to what she could

pretend was a date and it was… It was almost overwhelmingly exciting but terrifying
at the same time.

'You're very quiet tonight.' Josh sounded
sympathetic. 'I guess you're probably ex-
hausted from all the packing you're doing
on top of everything else.'

'Actually, I'm trying to remember the last
time I got taken out to dinner. And I've never
been to a Michelin-starred restaurant in my
life.'

'You look like you go out to places like
this all the time. Your dress is gorgeous and
that hairstyle is very elegant.'

'Thanks.' Stevie had to smile. 'It's just a
messy bun. There's not much I *can* do with
hair like mine. It has a personality all of its
own.'

Josh laughed. 'Like you,' he said, turning
to catch her gaze. 'I think you're both very
well suited.' He was slowing the vehicle. 'I
think we're here.'

'Wow…' Stevie took in the ivy-covered
stone walls of the old manor house and the
circular drive in front of it with a floodlit
fountain in a central garden. 'It looks amazing.'

'Mmm…' Josh shook his head. 'Don't

know how Lachlan swung it on such short notice. I'd heard that you needed a good percentage of royal blood or something to get a reservation here ever since it got its latest Michelin star.'

'Didn't you tell me that his father had been knighted? I'm guessing the name would be well known in these parts.' Stevie was watching Josh's face as he parked his car. 'Does it still bother you? That Lachlan grew up in such a different world?'

Again, Josh turned so that he could look at Stevie directly. 'You know what? I think I might have resented it a whole lot more if you hadn't put me straight.'

'Put you straight? How did I do that?'

'You made me realise that being so wealthy hasn't made Lachlan any happier than I am.'

Stevie felt a glow of pride that came from knowing that Josh had put such importance on something she'd said. She couldn't help the rebellious thought that followed almost instantly—that he might have a similar epiphany if she told him how she really felt about him. If she suggested that they could build a future together…

'To be honest,' Josh added, as he reached to open his door, 'I'm a bit worried about him. I think he's really struggling to get his head around having been adopted, so finding out he's got a brother has been more a shock to him than it is to me. He's not saying much, but I reckon he's lost weight over the last few weeks and he seems to look more stressed than ever now.'

'Maybe tonight will help.' Stevie followed his example and climbed out of the car.

She could help a little, too, by not disturbing Josh with any overly personal confessions. He had quite enough going on in his life and this wasn't *really* a date, was it? She might have indulged in a bit of a fantasy but she was really only here because Lachlan wanted to show his appreciation of how she'd sheltered the first meeting of these brothers. She smiled brightly at Josh as he arrived beside her to walk inside the restaurant. 'If nothing else, I'm sure the food will be extraordinary.'

The maître d' was waiting to welcome them, but also had a message to say that Mr McKendry had rung and he was running a little late.

'He asked that you be served a glass of champagne at the table while you're waiting. Please…follow me.'

If the menu was anything to go by, the food was certainly going to be nothing like Stevie had ever tasted. She and Josh read the items on the parchment paper while they sipped the champagne.

'Seafood risotto with squid ink?' Stevie whispered. 'And venison with blackberry brandy? Who thinks up combinations like that?'

'Foodies love it.' Josh smiled. 'And I read somewhere that the Cotswolds are rural England's foodie capital, but you know what?' There was something in his eyes that was melting something deep inside Stevie. He leaned closer and his words were only for her ears. 'I'm no foodie. I'd be just as happy with some of your mousetraps. Ah…that looks like Lachlan arriving now.'

Stevie was still smiling as she watched Josh's brother hand his coat to someone and then turn to help his companion remove hers. Stevie blinked.

'I thought he was bringing his mother's nurse?'

'He is.' Josh was also watching the way his brother was slipping that coat free from the shoulders of the rather gorgeous young woman with wavy blonde, shoulder-length hair. 'They do look like a couple,' he murmured. 'I wonder if that's something else he's not saying much about.'

The new arrivals hadn't noticed they were being watched yet and, as Lachlan turned to look for where his brother was seated, he also didn't notice the way his companion was looking up at him but Stevie recognised that look all too well. There was definitely something going on there. Something that made them a very close couple.

Her mouth suddenly went dry enough to make her reach for her water glass. Maybe tonight had the promise of being something even more than an hour or two of fantasy? It happened at weddings, didn't it? People who might be thinking that getting married was the last thing they wanted got unexpectedly coaxed into a very different direction. After thinking that they both shared a similar aversion to any kind of permanence in their relationships with women, if his brother really was in a meaningful relationship, could it change the shape of those boundaries he had in place around his own heart? Make a difference to how Josh felt about his own future, perhaps?

* * *

It was throwing him off balance a little, to be honest.

Josh hadn't expected Lachlan's mother's nurse to be such an attractive young woman. She had bright blue eyes in a classic combination with that blonde hair and she had a smile that was wide enough to be second only to Stevie's in the way it could light up a room.

'Call me Flick,' she'd told them the moment Lachlan had finished introducing her as Felicity. 'I've only ever been called Felicity by the taxman or the police.'

'What were the police after you for? No, don't tell me…' Lachlan was smiling. 'I think I'd rather leave that to my imagination for a while.'

Josh caught the ghost of a wink sent in his direction but it only added to that unsettled feeling. This was supposed to be an outing to thank both Flick and Stevie, wasn't it?

So why was it suddenly feeling like they were all on a double date?

That they were two couples seemed more obvious as they ordered their drinks and starters. Both Josh and Stevie chose stuffed Portobello mushrooms while Lachlan and

Flick both ordered hay-smoked scallops. It was a relief for Josh that the conversation turned in a more professional direction by the time those starters were served.

'How's that lad doing?' Lachlan asked Josh. 'From the brachial plexus repair?'

'Very well...' Josh was looking at Stevie, however, as he lifted another mouthful of the mushroom towards his mouth. He had been perfectly genuine in telling her how much he loved her mousetraps but these mushrooms were definitely to die for. Judging by the twinkle in her eyes, she was thinking along the same lines and it gave Josh an equally delicious frisson to know that they could have an entirely private moment like this when they were in such close company with other people.

'I've been trying to get back to see him again,' Lachlan added. 'But it's been full on.' He put down his fork, having barely tasted the scallops. 'Lectures here, surgeries there and I've had to dash up to London a couple of times as well.'

'Sounds stressful.' Josh could feel himself frowning. Was it all too much? Enough to be the reason why Lachlan was looking as if he'd lost weight? That he was too pale?

As if he could sense his brother's concern and wanted to brush it off, Lachlan was smiling brightly. 'At least I don't have to worry about anything on the home front.' He raised his glass in Flick's direction. 'You're doing a fabulous job,' he told her. 'I'm not at all surprised that London Locums considers you to be one their very best nurses. I will be grateful to you for ever. For everything...'

Flick dropped her gaze, seemingly embarrassed by the praise. Or was there some kind of hidden message there? A private moment, like the one he'd just had with Stevie? Whatever it was, it felt like distraction might be welcome.

'How long have you been doing locum nursing work, Flick?' Josh asked.

'Oh, years...' She looked up again to smile at him. 'I love the excitement of everything being new. Meeting new people, getting to know a new place. A new challenge...'

Lachlan made a sound that could have been suggesting that a 'challenge' might be an understatement in this case, but then became one of discomfort.

'It's a bit warm in here, isn't it?' He rubbed at a gleam of moisture on his forehead with his fingers, pushing it into his hairline, which made him look far less groomed than usual. Then he pushed back his chair. 'Excuse me for a moment. I just need a bit of fresh air.'

There was no mistaking the flash of real concern in Flick's eyes as Lachlan headed for a set of French doors near their table that led to a potager garden with strings of fairy lights woven into the low box hedges. She abandoned her own food and looked ready to go after him but Josh moved first.

'I'll go,' he said quietly.

The air was certainly a lot fresher outside but it didn't seem to be making an immediate difference to Lachlan, who was loosening his tie and undoing the top button of his shirt as Josh arrived by his side.

'You okay?'

'I'm fine.'

'You'd tell me if you weren't, wouldn't you?'

'Of course.' Lachlan's smile was a little too wide. 'You're my brother. Family, huh? *Real* family, that is…' He was staring in through the panes of the French doors to where Stevie and Flick were talking to each other. Because the fact that his mother's nurse was here was a reminder of the family he'd thought he'd had that *wasn't* real?

No…for a heartbeat there was something in Lachlan's gaze and his body language that Josh thought he could read only too well. It was enough to make him turn his own head to watch Stevie for a moment. To let himself feel that pull that was so strong it felt as if it could smash through any kind of barrier that was in the way.

It was so hard to imagine his life without Stevie in it now. Josh didn't *want* to imagine that. More than anything, he wanted to trust the extraordinary connection he'd found with Stevie. He would never have thought he'd actually be thinking in terms of a 'real' relationship but he couldn't deny that he was starting to. Something real enough that it could even lead to creating his own family?

But, then, he'd never expected to be presented with a real family member out of the blue, like this, either. The foundations of all those barriers Josh had built so many years ago appeared to be on rather shaky ground now. Was that something that Lachlan was also grappling with, perhaps? That might be contributing to the stress levels that were clearly affecting him?

'I think Flick's worried about you, too.'

'There's nothing to worry about,' Lachlan said. 'Not for you, and especially not for Flick. She's only here temporarily. Until I set up something permanent for my mother. Or put her in a home, perhaps. Which I might do any day now, the way things are going...'

'Maybe she would like to stay longer,' Josh suggested. 'I get the impression that you guys really like each other.'

He was speaking quietly, his gaze drawn back to Stevie, and it felt like he was saying his next words aloud for his own benefit— just to see what it felt like to explore this new, mind-bending idea.

'She might like the idea of something permanent herself,' he said. 'Maybe it's a shame if you don't hang on to something that's too good not to keep.'

Lachlan gave a huff of something like laughter as he pulled at his tie to take it off completely, except there was no amusement in the sound.

'Are you kidding? And here I was thinking that we were on the same page as far as women went. I mean, we both know that families aren't worth the effort and we both know why.'

'*We're* family now,' Josh said softly. He could understand exactly why Lachlan might be finding his feelings confusing. Overwhelming, even. Maybe it was something in common that could end up being the most important connection of all between them?

But Lachlan was turning away from the window. 'That's different,' he muttered. 'It's still time to move on the moment the girls get any ideas about anything permanent. A "future".' He made quotation marks with his fingers around the word. 'It's an "F" word as far as I'm concerned. Breaks all the…the…'

Lachlan never finished that sentence because he simply crumpled like an abandoned puppet and all Josh could do was to step in and break his fall. He caught his brother in his arms just before he hit the flagstone terrace.

He tilted Lachlan's head back to make sure his airway was open. Then he felt for a pulse in his neck, at the same time listening and feeling to see whether Lachlan was breathing. He felt the rush of warm air from the restaurant as the French doors were opened behind him and then Stevie and Flick were both there.

'What can I do?' Stevie asked.

'Oh, my God…' Flick dropped to her knees

beside Lachlan, her face as white as a sheet. *'No...'*

Josh caught Stevie's gaze. 'He's breathing,' he told her. 'And he's got a good, steady pulse. He may have just fainted for some reason but I think we'd better call an ambulance.'

The maître d' came through the doors in time to hear the end of his sentence. 'I've already taken care of that,' he said. 'They'll be here any minute.'

CHAPTER TEN

LACHLAN WAS CONSCIOUS by the time medical assistance arrived but his level of consciousness was down far enough to make him seem drowsy and his speech was a little incoherent so he'd been helped into the back of the ambulance to be assessed. The results from the ECG monitor, blood pressure check and oxygen saturation clip were normal enough not to cause concern.

'How much has he had to drink?' one of the paramedics asked.

'Not enough to do this,' Josh told them. 'I think there's something more going on here.'

'Gotta go home…' Lachlan tried to sit up. 'It's my mother… She's the one who's sick…'

'She's all right.' Flick was standing by the open back door of the ambulance. 'I just rang Mrs Tillman to tell her that I would be going to the hospital with you so I might be later than expected.'

But Lachlan was shaking his head. 'No need. I'm fine. And it's my mother you're employed to care for…not *me*… I don't need it… Can look after myself…'

Flick clearly tried to hide her reaction to his words but Josh could see they'd been hurtful.

'I'll go with Lachlan,' he told her. *Don't worry*, he tried to add silently. *He won't be alone.*

Flick nodded. 'I could take Stevie home, then.'

'No…that's in totally the opposite direction.' Josh turned to catch Stevie's gaze. He wanted to ask her to come with him as he accompanied his brother to Cheltenham Central, which would be the nearest hospital. He wanted her by his side as he waited to find out what, if anything, was wrong. But who knew how long that might take? She had to get home for Mattie.

'I'm going with Lachlan,' he said, to Stevie this time. 'I'll follow the ambulance in my car, so is it okay if I get a taxi to take you home?'

Stevie nodded. 'Of course.' She held his

gaze. 'Call me later—when you know what's going on?'

'It might be late.'

This time she shook her head. 'I'll still be up,' she told him. 'It doesn't matter how late it is.'

She was going to wait up for him to call.

Josh was smiling, even after the taxi had left and he was in his own vehicle ready to follow the ambulance.

It didn't matter that Stevie wasn't coming with him to share the wait and any news—good or bad. She was going to be waiting up for him and that was enough.

Oddly, it *felt* like she would be holding his hand, anyway.

Josh arrived at Cheltenham Central to find Lachlan in an observation area attached to the emergency department.

'They want to keep me in overnight.' Lachlan looked almost as pale as the pillows he was lying back against. 'I'd make a fuss and discharge myself but I'm… I'm just so damned tired, I don't want to move.'

'What do they think caused the syncope?'

'They're waiting for the blood results to come back. Consultant here thinks it could just be some kind of virus. I'm running a bit of a temperature and it fits with my not feeling so good in the last week or two.'

'What sort of "not so good"?' Josh could feel his frown deepen as he perched his hip on the end of Lachlan's bed. 'I did think you've been looking really tired. And you've lost some weight, too, haven't you?'

'A bit…' Lachlan closed his eyes. 'I've had some abdominal pain on and off so I haven't been eating much.' He managed a smile. 'And, hey…thanks for being here. Who knows, if I find I need a new kidney or something it could be really useful having a twin.'

Josh grinned back but the smile faded as he held his brother's gaze. He could actually feel the connection between them moving up a notch at this moment. Several notches. Had he really believed that he never needed or wanted family? This was his brother. His *identical* brother. It could be him lying in that bed and, if it was, he'd want family beside him.

It was Lachlan who broke the silence that had fallen.

'I was blaming how I felt on the stress of all the insanity of the last few weeks. I felt like someone had taken my life and turned it inside out. And upside down. And stomped on it. I was blindsided by finding out I'd been adopted. That the woman I thought was my mother had never wanted me in the first place. But finding out I've got a brother… well…that's a good thing.'

Josh nodded. He needed to swallow hard.

'And Flick…she's a good thing, too. You freaked me out back there by suggesting that it could be something permanent, mind you.'

'I get that.' Josh sighed. 'I think I freaked myself out a bit as well. I'd actually started thinking—'

He didn't get a chance to confess that he was starting to change his own mind about that aversion to permanence, thanks to how he felt about Stevie, because the curtain around Lachlan's bed opened.

'Hope I'm not interrupting anything. I'm Graham—a consultant here.' The newcomer held his hand out to Josh. 'Wow… I've heard about you two but you really are identical, aren't you?'

'I'm the better-looking twin,' Lachlan said. 'You've probably heard that, as well.'

Josh could see that, behind the attempt at humour, Lachlan had become very still. He was looking at the paper the consultant was holding in his hands and Graham's smile had vanished by the time he spoke again.

'You've got something going on, Lachlan,' he said. 'Your blood count's all over the place. White blood count's way up and red cells and platelets are low enough to be concerning.'

Josh actually felt a chill ripple down his spine. He'd seen blood results like that come in on children all too often. He might have referred those patients to the oncology team instantly but he was often there as the parents were given the devastating news that their child had leukaemia.

Lachlan had joined the dots as quickly as Josh had. He could see the shock in his eyes, even though he was doing his best to hide it.

'Not just a virus, then?'

Graham could see that both the doctors in front of him knew exactly how serious this could prove to be. 'We've already lined up some more tests for first thing tomorrow.'

'Do they include a bone-marrow biopsy?' Lachlan asked quietly.

Graham nodded. 'I've already been in touch with the team you'll be admitted under. The HOD of Haematology is a great guy.

He's offered to come in and have a chat with you tonight, if you'd like.'

But Lachlan shook his head. 'I'm really tired,' he said. 'I think I'd rather get some sleep.'

Josh was still sitting on the end of the bed when the emergency department consultant left. The shock was still there but he knew how to keep it from showing in his voice.

'Can I get you anything?'

'No, thanks.' Lachlan didn't open his eyes as he spoke. 'You should get home. That dog of yours probably needs to get outside.'

'I can stay for a while.' Josh didn't want to leave his brother alone. His own mind was racing fast enough as it gathered the implications of what they'd been told. 'If you want to talk.'

But Lachlan turned away. 'Go home, Josh,' he muttered. 'I just need to sleep.'

'I'll be back tomorrow, then.' Josh hesitated as he turned towards the door, however. He was pretty sure Lachlan was not about to go to sleep but his brother clearly wanted to be alone.

Because, like Josh, he'd spent his life having to deal with the tough stuff alone?

'Just call if you want to,' he added softly,

his fingers curling around the phone in his pocket. 'Anytime.'

He had the phone in his hand by the time he got back to where he'd parked his car. It was almost a shock to realise that it was only a matter of a few hours since he'd had Stevie sitting in the passenger seat and they'd been on their way to a fabulous restaurant. Before his life had been derailed—*again*.

He wished she was sitting there right now. He wanted to tell her how afraid he was that Lachlan was seriously ill. And he could do that. She was, after all, waiting up for him to call but, if he started, where would he stop? Would he just let it all come rushing out? Tell her that he was scared that maybe he'd discovered he had a brother only to have to face losing him?

That he would tell her how much he'd wanted to have Stevie holding his hand for company and support tonight. That he wanted her to tell him that it was all going to be okay. That he wanted to feel her arms around him. To hear her say that, even if it wasn't all going to be okay, she'd be right there beside him.

That he would never need to be alone again.

But…what if she didn't say that? If she didn't feel that way? It wasn't as if they had a definitive diagnosis for Lachlan yet, either. That would come tomorrow, probably after a raft of more focused investigations, and he would be seeing Stevie at work so there would be plenty of time to talk. Maybe the weather would be nice enough to have lunch on the roof? It was a shame they'd missed everything other than the starter at that posh restaurant.

Josh didn't put his phone away, though, even after he was sitting inside his car. He found Stevie's number and sent her a text.

No real news yet. Talk to you tomorrow when we get more test results. Maybe we could meet for lunch?

Her response was so quick she must have had her phone in her hand already.

Sure. See you tomorrow. Sleep well.

It was time Josh put his phone down and headed for home but he wasn't quite ready to move. He opened a browser and found a site that he relied on for accurate and up-to-date medical articles.

Adult onset leukaemia, he typed into the search bar. *Diagnosis, treatment and prognosis.*

Gloucester General's rooftop vegetable garden seemed to have become the background setting that marked milestones in Stevie Hawksbury's new life. It had been where the aftermath of that awkward first meeting with her boss had been smoothed over enough to be forgotten. Where they'd shared secrets and cemented the first foundation stones of their friendship in place.

It was where so many private conversations had taken place in snatched minutes of shared lunches. It had been one of those conversations that had persuaded her that Mattie was old enough to travel alone to visit his grandma and she was still seeing the benefits of the independence and confidence that weekend had given him. Or maybe it was her son's relationship with his Big Brother mentor that was making it seem like Mattie was growing more mature and grounded day by day.

It had been the weekend of that independent trip that had been one of the biggest milestones of all—when she and Josh had made love for the first time. Another ripple from the stone that had been cast on the day that Josh had brought her up here to these gardens. She loved coming here. Except that, today, Stevie was barely aware of where they were. All she could think about was how pale and drawn Josh was looking when he arrived. All she wanted was to put her arms around him and hold him as tightly as she could.

All she did, however, was to pass him the plastic triangle that contained the sandwiches she'd bought at the cafeteria, although she let her hand brush his and their eye contact to linger for a heartbeat. She knew there was a group of junior doctors sitting not that far away, having also chosen to take their lunch break where they could find a bit of sunshine and, even though Josh had been happy to take her out to a famous local restaurant last night and it had felt almost like a date to start with, at least, Stevie was quite sure he wouldn't want rumours about them to start circulating around the hospital. Especially not today, when he looked tired enough for it to be too much effort to even open that plastic triangle.

'Did you stay with Lachlan all night?' she asked.

'No. He told me to go home. Said he needed to sleep but I think he just wanted to be alone. I was there this morning, though. I was with him when he got the results of his bone-marrow biopsy.'

Stevie had opened her own sandwich container but any appetite for lunch evaporated instantly on hearing those words. She felt fear, she realised. For Lachlan. But even more for Josh because she could see her fear reflected in his eyes and she could feel the painful cracking in her own heart. She didn't need to ask the question.

'It's AML,' he said quietly. 'Acute myeloid leukaemia.'

'Oh… God…' Stevie totally forgot about anyone who could see them. She put her hand over Josh's and held on.

'We both had our suspicions last night,' Josh continued. 'After the results of the blood count came through and we added up all the other symptoms, like extreme fatigue recently and odd bruising and a fever and so on. The ED consultant even said that the haematology consultant was prepared to come in and talk to Lachlan right there and then but the diagnosis wasn't official until the results of this morning's biopsy came through.' Josh closed his eyes as he rubbed his forehead. 'There should be less than five percent of blasts in bone marrow—they're the immature white blood cells. Lachlan's got more than twenty percent.'

Stevie swallowed hard. 'I'm so sorry,' she whispered. 'How's Lachlan coping?'

Josh seemed to squeeze his eyes even more tightly shut. As if he was staving off tears?

'The first thing he said was that I'd better get myself tested. That if there was a genetic component to being at risk then I might be next.'

The wash of fear that Stevie had felt only minutes ago came back so fiercely that she instinctively broke the skin contact between her hand and Josh's in case he could feel it too. But the words came out before she could stop them and it felt all too obvious that she was afraid.

'That's not true,' she breathed. And then she caught the corner of her lip between her teeth. 'Is it?'

Josh opened his eyes and turned towards

Stevie. He wasn't smiling, but the crinkles at the corners of his eyes deepened, as if he appreciated that she was so concerned about him.

'Funnily enough, when I was sitting up all night, reading up on every type of leukaemia I could think of, I came across a fairly recent article about identical twins getting diagnosed with AML within days of each other. Concordant AML, it's called...'

'And...?' Stevie couldn't bear the pause.

'They were just kids.' But Josh found a lopsided smile. 'But they had a sibling who was an HLA match and they got a stem cell transplant, which has apparently cured them. They didn't even get any GVHD.'

'GVHD?'

'Graft versus host disease. It's a common complication with any kind of transplant that can be serious. It often goes away after a year or so but the better HLA match you can get, the less risk there is of getting it in the first place. HLA is human leukocyte antigens.' He let his breath out in a long sigh. 'I think I reviewed my entire haematology course between about four and six this morning.'

The cracks in Stevie's heart deepened. She wished she'd been there for Josh. To bring him something to eat or just coffee. To talk things through. Just…to *be* there…

'I will get myself tested,' Josh added. 'Not to see if I've got anything abnormal going on in my blood. To see if I'm going to be the perfect match to donate my bone marrow for the transplant.' That crooked smile was back. 'And, if anybody should be the perfect match, it's got to be an identical twin.'

'That must have helped.' Stevie said. 'To tell Lachlan that.'

'I haven't told him yet.'

'How come?'

'It got mentioned, of course, but it's down the track and there's some rough stuff to get through before a stem cell transplant is going to be on the agenda. The focus right now is on getting more information about the sub-type and staging and planning the chemo-therapy regime that needs to start as soon as possible. Hopefully tomorrow. And…' The expression on Josh's face was a silent groan.

Stevie hadn't thought her heart could sink much further but she'd been wrong. 'And what?'

'There was other stuff happening. Between Lachlan and Flick. She was there this morning, as well. You should have seen her face, Stevie.' Josh had to stop talking. He took a deep breath and then cleared his throat. 'She looked like the world was ending. Said she was so sorry but she couldn't do this again. And then she walked out of the room.'

'*Again?*'

'Lachlan told me later that her husband had died—a long time ago now—from pancreatic cancer. Six weeks from diagnosis to death and she never left his side. It broke her, he said. She's been running ever since.'

'But I saw the way she looked at him,' Stevie said softly. 'And we were talking while you were outside with Lachlan at the restaurant. I know she's in love with him.'

As much as *she* was in love with Josh…

'Well…she can't face this.'

Stevie was quite sure of what she knew about how Flick felt. How powerful did the shadow of her past have to be to make her walk out at a time like that? How devastating that must have been for Lachlan. And for Josh to be there and witness what could have been a sudden end to his brother's relationship.

'How did Lachlan take it?'

Josh was rubbing his forehead again with

his middle finger, as if the touch might reduce the discomfort of his thoughts.

'He kind of shrugged it off. Said he didn't blame her, after what she'd been through. But you could see that it hurt. I told him I'd be sticking around but...you know what?'

Stevie didn't say anything. She just held his gaze.

'I hate myself for saying it but I get why she's running.'

'I know. I can't even imagine how hard this is for her. Or for you. But it's so lucky you've found each other—you and Lachlan.'

'Is it?' Josh broke the eye contact by closing his eyes. 'Yes, of course it is. I'm just... It gets me—here...' He put his hand on his chest. 'And I don't think I've felt like this about anyone since I was a little kid. I've never let myself feel like this because I know what happens. I know this isn't Lachlan's fault but the end result could be the same.' His voice was so quiet it felt like Josh was talking aloud to himself. 'There are no guarantees in life. You can't trust that anyone's going to hang around for ever. Or even for the important stuff.'

'Sometimes you can.' The cracks in Stevie's heart were wide enough to be breaking her heart, knowing that Josh had gone through his life not trusting enough to let himself love someone. Or to *be* loved by someone. 'I'm not going anywhere, Josh.'

'Thanks…' Josh was looking down at the plastic container he was still holding. 'And thanks for getting lunch but… I don't think I can eat right now. I need to get going, too. I've got to catch up on the ward round I missed this morning.'

'Take them with you. Try and find time to eat later. It's not going to help you or Lachlan if you don't look after yourself.'

Josh nodded, getting slowly to his feet.

'And I'll tell Mattie that you won't be able to make his Big Brother session this week.'

'No…don't do that.' Josh straightened, taking a deep breath. 'That's important, too.'

'He'll understand.'

Josh shook his head. 'He might seem like he's growing up really fast at the moment but he's still just a kid on the inside and I don't want to let him down. And, hey…it'll be good for me, too. We'll go somewhere nice with Lucky and forget about the rest of the world for a while.'

'Oh…that reminds me.' Stevie was on her feet now as well. She would find time to eat her sandwich later—although it didn't seem likely that she was going to feel hungry anytime soon. 'Mattie wanted me to talk to you about when Lucky's going to move in. He's got this idea that he wants him to sleep on the end of his bed the first night we're in the cottage but I said that it might need to wait until we're a bit more settled in.'

'Okay.' Josh was smiling. 'Sounds like he's excited about the move.'

'We both are. I should warn you that he knows you've got a brother you didn't know you had. He's probably going to have a million questions about that, too. Sorry...'

'I'll cope.' Josh's face had softened and he stood there for a moment, just holding Stevie's gaze. Looking for all the world as if he wanted to kiss her...

And, suddenly, it didn't matter who might be watching or what sort of rumours might circulate. Josh might believe that he didn't need anything more than a friendship from her but what he actually needed more than anything right now was to know that he had someone who cared about him. Who was going to do everything they could to help him through whatever he was about to face.

Stevie closed the gap between them and

put her arms up to offer him a hug and, to her relief, he didn't seem at all bothered that other people might see them. He leaned down and let himself be hugged and Stevie held him as tightly as she could. So tightly she could feel the beat of both their hearts. It felt like he was even letting go of some of the tension in his body, just for a heartbeat or two—but it was enough.

Hopefully, it was enough to let him know everything he needed to know.

CHAPTER ELEVEN

THE SKILLS OF being able to compartmentalise and focus purely on what was in that particular compartment had never been more valuable. And, man... Josh had needed to call on those skills in the last day or two.

He was using them now as he stood beside the trolley that contained all the patient notes for children who were currently inpatients. He was anxious to find out what had happened since he'd seen one of his young patients on this morning's ward round. Four-year-old Jayden had managed to stick the prong of a fork far enough into a wall plug to receive a significant electrical shock. His panicked mother had rushed him into Emergency and he'd then been admitted to hospital for treatment to burns on his fingers, hand and chest and observation for an irregular heartbeat that was potentially of concern.

Today Josh had requested both surgical and cardiology consults and he was scanning Jayden's notes to find out the latest results of any new investigations. He was relieved to note that today's observations were normal for temperature, blood pressure, oxygen saturation and GCS. Blood test results were also normal. The daily dressing change for the burns had gone well and the current pain management was adequate. A note had been made that a plastic surgery consult should be arranged in case of possible grafting needed to one fingertip but even that didn't dent Josh's focus.

He was more interested in the results of the echocardiogram that had been done this afternoon and the new ECG in the series that had been requested. The irregular rhythm had been caused by premature beats in the atria of the heart but they seemed to be settling now and the cardiology team was confident the abnormality would resolve soon.

Josh breathed out a sigh of relief at this point and finally allowed a breach in the wall of the mental compartment he'd been in for some hours now that didn't allow anything other than a focus on his patients. He let his gaze drift back to the section in Jayden's notes where the surgical team had suggested a referral to a more specialist area. Lachlan's specialty. The longing that it could have been possible to call his brother in to review the case was so strong it was a physical pain in his chest and, as Josh slotted Jayden's notes back into the trolley, he closed his eyes and took a deep breath to try and counteract that pain.

He was lucky he had different compartments he could use right now, like his work and his responsibilities to a small, white dog who needed walks and food. Lachlan didn't have the luxury of any kind of distractions and, after the initial shock, the reality of his situation had sunk in with what threatened to be a devastating effect. When Josh had gone to see him last night, Lachlan had pretty much ordered him not to continue his visits.

Josh kept his eyes closed for another moment as their conversation flashed through the back of his mind while he searched for the exact wording that had haunted a restless night and been forced under cover while he'd been working through an exceptionally busy day today.

'You don't have to be here. I know I'm not exactly good company.'

'I want to be here.'

'You managed without me in your life for thirty-six years, Josh. It won't be that hard to get used to it again.'

'I don't want to get used to it. You're my brother. The only family I've got.'

'You might have to get used to it.'

There'd been no amusement at all in Lachlan's huff of laughter.

'Take a leaf out of Flick's book. She's managed to walk away, no problem.'

'Has she? Has she actually gone?'

'Well...she's still here—in the district, at least. But only until we can find another locum nurse. My housekeeper, Mrs Tillman, is sorting that mess out for me. You're not going to believe this, but she says Josephine is upset about me. Crocodile tears, huh?'

'I doubt that. Sometimes it takes a shock for people to wake up and see what really matters.'

'Well... I've had a shock and...guess what? Nothing really matters. Go away, Josh. Get on with your own life. Get over yourself and marry that nice girl with that astonishing hair.'

Lachlan had even found a smile, although it hadn't lasted long.

'Go. Be happy for both of us...'

It had been a knee-jerk reaction to the shock of a frightening diagnosis, which had been made all the more confronting by having already had his life turned upside down by recent developments. Josh wasn't about to give up on supporting his brother, however. In fact, perhaps he could go over to Cheltenham Central right now and still have time to be back in town to meet Mattie at the Big Brother Headquarters, as usual, at four-thirty p.m.

A twist of his wrist revealed the face of his watch but it was clearly incorrect. He reached into his pocket for his phone only to find that he'd forgotten to charge it last night and it was completely dead. Josh turned away from the trolley to look at the wall clock in the ward's reception area and it was then that he simply froze.

It was six p.m. How on earth could that possibly have happened? He'd never even been late to meet Mattie for their weekly session together on a Thursday, let alone completely forgotten about it. Stevie had suggested it could be cancelled, hadn't she? She'd known he had too much going at the moment but he'd refused. What had he said to her? Oh, yeah…that their time together was important, too. That Mattie might seem like he was growing up really fast but he was still just a kid on the inside. He'd also said that he didn't want to let him down.

Worse than that, Josh had promised Stevie long ago that he'd never do anything to hurt Mattie.

Oh… God… He had to try and put this right.

Right now…

Stevie knew who it was before she even opened the door of her apartment to find Josh standing there.

She also knew there had to be a very good reason that Josh had not shown up for his session with Mattie this afternoon but, no matter how good that reason was and how apologetic Josh was looking, it wasn't likely to be enough. Not this time.

'I'm *so* sorry,' he said. 'I completely lost track of time.'

That was it? No major emergency in the ward? No new development that had been serious enough for him to have had to rush to his brother's side? He'd just…*forgotten* about Mattie?

'He tried to walk home after he'd waited for you for more than an hour,' Stevie said. 'And you know what? That gang of boys he'd had trouble with when we first moved here were waiting for him when he got close to home.'

'Oh… God, *no*…' Josh's eyes looked even darker as his face paled. 'Is he hurt?'

'He's got a few bruises. Had his schoolbag stolen…' Stevie had to swallow hard before she could continue without her voice breaking. 'Mostly, he just got terrified.'

'Can I come in?' Josh's voice was raw. 'And talk to Mattie?'

Stevie wasn't at all sure she could cope with having Josh too close right now. Her head was all over the place. Her heart felt like it was breaking.

'It's a mess in here,' she said. 'There's barely room to move with all the packing boxes and piles of stuff.' She turned her head away from him. 'Mattie? Can you come here for a minute?'

Mattie's bedroom door was the closest one to the front door. Even if he hadn't guessed who had come calling, he would have heard Josh's voice.

'Don't want to,' he responded. 'I'm busy.'

Playing an online game, Stevie suspected. The way he'd spent far too much time doing when they'd first moved to Gloucester.

'Please?' Stevie didn't raise her voice. Mattie knew the tone she was using well enough to understand that this was something important. And, a few seconds later, he appeared outside his bedroom door to stand in this narrow hallway. He didn't look at Josh, though. He was staring at his feet.

'I'm so sorry, Mattie,' Josh said again. 'I'll make it up to you, I promise.'

Mattie said nothing. He didn't look up, either.

'Tomorrow,' Josh offered. 'I've got a day off. How 'bout we go and check out your new village and see where the best places are going to be to walk Lucky?'

Mattie shrugged. 'Whatever...'

He stepped back into his room and pushed the door shut behind him. It wasn't quite a slam that would have required a response from Stevie but it was certainly firm enough to be a warning that he was done with communicating for now.

Josh looked at Stevie as if he was expecting her to fix this somehow but that wasn't going to happen, was it? This had become too big and Stevie was being pulled in two very different directions.

'Why didn't you call, Josh? Or send a text or something? I could have gone and walked home with him. Made sure he wasn't going to blame you for this.'

'My phone was dead. I meant to charge it last night but I fell asleep on the couch. I'd been trying to read up on all the latest clinical trials for AML. Look, I'm sorry I've upset Mattie. I'm beyond sorry that he ran into trouble. You know that, don't you?'

Of course she did. Like she'd known there would be a good reason behind what had happened. Too many good reasons but that didn't alter the fact that her son felt betrayed. Like he didn't matter enough. This was tearing her apart more than she'd thought it would. She knew what Josh was going through and she wanted to support him in whatever way he needed but…this was *Mattie* they were talking about. Her precious son. The boy she'd based her life around ever since he'd been conceived. The boy they'd both promised they would never do anything to hurt. Now Josh had let him down and Stevie hadn't been able to do anything to protect him.

'He's not just upset,' she said. 'He's really

hurt, Josh. You're way more important than you probably realise in his life. You're far more like a father figure than a big brother for Mattie and he *trusted* you. You've let him down and…and you promised you'd never do that. That you'd never hurt him.'

Josh was rubbing his forehead in that characteristic gesture of trying to collect or redefine his thoughts.

'This is what happens, isn't it?' he muttered. 'You get close to people. When you trust them and you let them trust you. And then people get hurt.'

Stevie had the sensation of the walls closing in around her. There seemed to be a lot less oxygen in the air as well. This was it, wasn't it? The barrier that Josh had always used to keep himself safe. Was he about to reinstate it? With her and Mattie on the other side? She couldn't let that happen. It didn't matter if she got hurt but it sure as hell mattered if Mattie did.

'You can't just walk out on him,' she said slowly. 'You must know how much that would hurt him.'

'Of course I do.' But Josh shook his head. 'It was a mistake, wasn't it? I should never have got involved in the first place. He can't think of me as his dad, Stevie. I'm *not*.' He was turning away. 'You know perfectly well that I never wanted to be *anybody's* dad.'

The crack in Stevie's heart opened wide enough to be a potentially fatal wound. 'Just go,' she told him.

She couldn't cope with this while Josh was standing this close to her. The idea that he was about to push her out of his life was bad enough but that he thought his relationship with Mattie had been a mistake was beyond heartbreaking. How on earth was she ever going to explain this to Mattie? It had been easy to make sure he didn't know about the rejection from his biological father but this was on a very different level. The amount of damage this could do was scary. She would have to cope with what might be the hardest challenge she'd ever faced but she needed time to think about how she was even going to start. And she needed to do it alone because Mattie wasn't about to listen to anything else that Josh might have to say.

She lifted her chin. 'I'll deal with this.' She bit the words out. 'I have to, because I don't get a choice about being a parent or not. I'm Mattie's mother and that's never going to change. I don't *want* it to change.' She pulled in a new breath. 'We don't need your help. We don't need *you...*'

Josh still looked as though he had no intention of going, so Stevie helped him out. She shut the door in his face.

She didn't try and open Mattie's door because she knew it would only make things worse if she forced him to talk to her before he was ready. She wasn't ready, either, so it was just as well she had a whole lot of packing to finish in the kitchen before she could even start cooking dinner.

Stevie did tap on Mattie's door, however. 'It's going to be okay, Mattie,' she called softly. 'I promise.' She bit her lip. 'I'll call you when dinner's ready.'

It took longer than she'd thought to finish wrapping all the glassware and plates in newspaper and stacking them into boxes. And then she heated up the oven and unwrapped a frying pan she'd already packed by mistake.

'There'll be no more fish fingers or chips or fried eggs once we've moved,' she told herself. 'It's going to be a new life and we're going to make it work.'

They had to and that was all there was to it.

This time, Stevie opened Mattie's door after she'd knocked on it.

'Dinner's ready,' she said. 'Come and wash your hands.'

There was no response to her instruction.

Because Mattie wasn't there…

In that moment of time, seconds before Stevie knew she would be frantically calling for her son and checking the bathroom and living room and Mrs Johnson's apartment and the stairwell of the building, she knew she wasn't going to find him.

She could sense the emptiness…

And that was when the fear stepped in…

CHAPTER TWELVE

THE CLOSING OF that door felt like a slap in the face.

A dismissal.

He wasn't wanted here, was he?

He took the stairs to get out of this apartment block because he needed the movement. Not that it stopped his brain raking through everything, mind you, but at least it felt like he was pushing through it by moving. It would be worse to be standing still inside an elevator, letting it smother him. Seeing that expression on Mattie's face when he'd turned away from Josh had taken him straight back to his own childhood. To when those feelings of being let down had been sharp enough to cut so deeply.

He hated that he'd let Mattie down. More than that, he admitted as he hit the street and headed to his car. He'd hurt him badly and Stevie had every right to be angry with him but it hadn't been intentional. He had way too much going on at the moment, that was all. And, because he'd needed to shut out the overwhelming worry about Lachlan so he could do his job, he'd ended up shutting out too much—to the point of forgetting something even when he knew how important it was.

Josh sat in his car for a minute, looking up at the floor that was probably the one where Stevie and Mattie's apartment was. Should he go back? Try and explain?

No. He turned the key and started the engine. He had to get home. He didn't know if Lucky had even been let out this afternoon and the little dog's dinner was overdue as well. He added that concern to everything else and it was, possibly, the straw that was about to break the camel's back.

The mix of the level of worry he'd already been dealing with from the moment he'd known that his brother was sick along with the remorse that had sent him rushing to apologise to Mattie and Stevie was coagulating into a much harsher emotion.

Anger.

Not with Lachlan for being sick. Or Mattie for being hurt. Or even Stevie for pushing him away like that. He understood. Of course he understood. Josh knew exactly why this was all going so very wrong. He'd broken the rules. He'd let himself get too close to others and he'd let others get too close to him. And now people were getting hurt. Including himself. The way he'd been hurt—too often—when he'd been too young to defend himself. The way he'd vowed that he would never let happen again.

He left the outskirts of Gloucester behind and headed towards the outlying villages along winding roads and gave in to beating himself up.

Why on earth had he thought it was a good idea to join the Big Brother organisation when it was painfully obvious he was going to get close to whatever kid he developed a relationship with? Especially one who had reminded him so much of himself as a kid?

He'd let himself get far too close to Stevie, as well. Had he really believed he could keep the kind of distance from her that he'd managed to hang on to in every one of his previous relationships with women? Stevie was nothing like any of those women. The connection they had was like nothing he'd even believed existed.

Lucky was overjoyed to see Josh as he arrived home and he was also desperate to get out into the garden. Josh got the little dog's dinner ready but wasn't tempted at all by the idea of eating anything himself. He went to pour himself a small whisky instead, but the sight of the bottle that he and Lachlan had all but emptied on that night they'd sat up talking till all hours gave Josh another kick in the guts.

Was this the worst thing of all right now?

That he'd found he had *family*? A brother? Not just any sibling either, but a twin. An identical twin, which was the closest kind of genetic relationship it was possible to have. They'd only known of each other's existence for a short time but already it was like catching glimpses of a part of himself he hadn't known was missing.

It was something precious.

And it was under threat. Breaking something deep inside him. Blowing holes in any carefully crafted defence systems and…and it *hurt*, dammit.

Lucky had finished his dinner and was

trying to stay as close to Josh as possible as he paced around his house.

'I'm not going to let him do it,' he told the dog. 'I'm not going to let him push me away like that. He might not like the idea of needing someone any more than I do but that's just the way it is.' Whatever journey was waiting for his brother, he wasn't going to be taking it alone.

He punched in the rapid dial number on his phone and listened to it ring. And then he listened to Lachlan's voice telling him he wasn't available and inviting him to leave a message.

Josh hung up instead. Then he looked down at the little white dog. 'I'm going to the hospital,' he said. 'Want a ride in the car?'

His phone rang as he fastened his seat belt and he answered it without even glancing at the screen, assuming it was Lachlan returning his call.

But it wasn't his brother. It was Stevie.

'I was wrong, Josh.' They were her first words. 'We *do* need you…'

The fear in her voice broke his heart wide open. He might be getting glimpses of a part of himself that he hadn't known was missing when it came to his twin brother but it was at that moment that Josh realised Stevie was an even bigger part of his life that had been missing. He couldn't not love her. He couldn't allow her to be frightened, either. Not if there was anything he could do about that.

'I'm on my way,' he told Stevie. 'What's happened, darling?'

'It's Mattie.' He could hear the strangled sob in her voice. 'He's run away…'

Having Josh with her didn't make it any less terrifying for Stevie that Mattie had run away but as she stood beside his car, wrapped in his arms, she knew that it was the only thing that could have provided any kind of anchor in this totally unexpected and unbelievably scary maelstrom.

'This is my fault,' she told Josh. 'I knew he was upset but I just left him alone. I was packing crockery and pots and things in the kitchen because I thought the best thing I could do was to make sure we moved as soon as possible. That I got him away from that gang of boys that had scared him.' She took in a shaky breath. 'I was making so much noise it's no wonder I didn't hear him sneak out of the apartment.'

'We're going to find him,' Josh said, softly. 'And I don't think I'm going to let either of you out of my sight ever again.'

They were words that Stevie might have been dreaming of hearing but right now they just floated over her head and evaporated into the night.

'Let's go,' she said.

'Where, first?'

'I don't know.' Stevie climbed into the Jeep. 'Anywhere we can think of. I just need to be going *somewhere*. Doing *something*.'

The police had agreed that Stevie and Josh should go and search for Mattie. Mrs Johnson from next door would be keeping watch and would let them know if Mattie returned home. He hadn't been missing long enough to justify a full-scale police operation, especially since he was old enough to be able to hide effectively if that was what he intended to do. The police would keep an eye out in the area, of course, and they'd have a word with that gang of boys that were known to be causing a bit of havoc locally.

'Where would he go?' Josh wondered aloud. 'Who would he want to talk to if he was upset?'

'His gran,' Stevie said.

'Maybe he's headed for the station, where he caught the bus that time to go and see her. Do you know if he's called her?'

Stevie shook her head. 'She would have called me if he had. I don't want to tell her what's happened just yet. I don't want to worry her, in case it turns out to be nothing...'

Josh was heading for the central city but he glanced at the sign indicating the direction to take a motorway out of town. 'He wouldn't be trying to get to your new house, by any chance? Or mine—to see Lucky, maybe?'

Hearing his name, Lucky sat up on the back seat and wagged his tail but, again, Stevie shook her head.

'He doesn't even know the name of the village yet.' But she turned to look at Lucky again, reaching out to pat the little dog. 'He does love Lucky, though.'

'We're not that far from the vet clinic we went to a couple of times. He loved being there and helping with Lucky's care.'

'He did.' Stevie found a wobbly smile. 'That was the first time I'd seen him looking really happy since we'd moved here. Lucky—and you—made such a difference for us.'

Josh had slowed the car and then stopped. 'The park here. This is where we brought Lucky on our first official Big Brother session. When we had to take turns carrying him because he couldn't walk yet.'

They both got out of the car and walked a little way along the path. Josh was holding Stevie's hand and she was holding his so tightly he was losing sensation in his fingers.

'Mattie!' Stevie shouted. 'Are you here?'

'Mattie...' Josh echoed her call. 'Where are you, mate?'

They stood there, listening to the silence coming from the dark shadows in the park.

'He's not here,' Stevie whispered. 'I can feel it. Just like I could feel that he wasn't in the apartment. It's just too...empty...'

'I know.' Josh squeezed her hand.

Stevie rested her head against his shoulder to take a deep breath. 'Thank you,' she murmured.

'What for?'

'Being here.'

'Where else would I be?' Josh turned his head so that he could capture her gaze. 'I love you, Stevie. And I love Mattie.'

Oh...the look in his eyes. This wasn't the kind of love that came with a friendship.

This was the soul-deep, one-of-a-kind love that could connect two people for a lifetime. The kind of love that Stevie had tried—and failed—not to have for Josh. But she could only focus on his last words. That he loved Mattie.

'He adores *you*,' she told Josh. She had to swallow hard to fight back tears. 'When you asked who he'd want to talk to? That would be you, even more than his gran. Maybe he felt bad about not talking to you when you came to apologise for missing the session today. He might be trying to find you.'

'But he doesn't know where I live.'

'He knows where he's always found you, though. Every Thursday.'

'The Big Brother Headquarters.' Josh was looking over Stevie's head. 'It's just down the road. Come on…'

This part of the inner city was much quieter in the evenings and the wide street was almost deserted. Josh drove slowly and then pulled up close to the building they both recognised.

'Spooky place at this time of night,' he said. 'Surely he wouldn't come here?'

But there was a shadow on the wide step in front of the door. At first glance it looked like a rubbish bag. Or a pile of old clothing, perhaps, but on closer inspection it became obvious that it was a small person, hunched up, with their head cradled on their arms.

Stevie and Josh were out of the car at exactly the same moment. They even spoke at exactly the same time and in exactly the same tone of absolute relief.

'*Mattie...*'

For the longest time the three of them sat on that step together. Stevie was on one side of Mattie and Josh was on the other and they both had an arm around him.

A Mattie sandwich.

There was a street lamp nearby, which gave more than enough light for them to be able to look at each other over the top of Mattie's head. To hold that eye contact long enough to be absolutely sure that there were promises being made. Maybe the exact wording of those promises would have to wait for a whispered conversation when they were alone in each other's arms but, for now, this was enough.

More than enough.

Stevie had never felt this happy. Ever.

'Oh,' she finally said aloud. 'We'd better

let the police know they can stop looking for Mattie.'

'I left my phone in the car,' Josh said.

'I'll do it.' Stevie dialled the number she'd been given and it was a quick message to impart.

Mattie was looking up at her when she'd finished. 'Were the police really looking for me?'

'Of course they were. I had no idea where you were.' Stevie's voice wobbled. 'You scared me, Mattie.'

'Sorry, Mum…' Mattie ducked his head and reached to stroke Lucky, who was sitting quietly on his feet, pressed as close as he could get to his favourite person.

'Why did you run away, mate?' Josh's query was gentle.

'I heard you.' Mattie gulped in a huge breath. 'I heard you say that you weren't my dad…'

He still had his head down, focused on Lucky, so it was only Stevie who could see how genuine the apology in Josh's eyes was.

'I'm really sorry, Mattie,' he said. 'I know it's not much of an excuse but I'd had a bad day. A bad week, in fact. Did you know that I've got a brother I didn't even know I had?'

'Yeah… Mum told me. How come you didn't know?'

'It's a bit of a long story that I'll tell you soon. Bottom line was that we got given to different families when we were born because our mum didn't want us. Or couldn't look after us, maybe. She can't have been as brave as your mum.'

Mattie finally looked up at Josh. 'That's really cool,' he said. 'To have a brother. *I'd* like a brother. Or a sister, even…' Then he sighed heavily. 'But Mum can't have another baby.'

'Oh?' Stevie blinked. 'Why not?'

'Because you don't even have a boyfriend, Mum.'

'Yes, she does.' Josh spoke quietly but with absolute conviction. 'Your mum has a boyfriend who loves her very, very much.'

'But you said,' Mattie insisted. 'You said you didn't want to be my dad. That you never want to be anybody's dad.'

Stevie held her breath as the silence stretched. She watched the way Josh tilted his head until it was almost touching Mattie's. As if this was a private conversation.

'I only said that because I was scared,' he said, very quietly. 'If I was going to be anybody's dad, in the whole wide world, I'd want it to be you.'

Mattie's voice was almost inaudible. 'Why?'

'Because I love you,' Josh responded. 'Like the way I love your mum. Which means it's never going to disappear. Ever…'

He looked up and the touch of that eye contact was like a hug. A promise all on its own. Stevie had to blink away tears that were just part of this enormous happiness.

'Really?' Mattie was staring at Josh intently.

'Really.'

Mattie sucked in another big breath. He was leaning towards Josh now and he lowered his voice. This was also private.

'You *could* be my dad,' he whispered. 'If you married my mum.'

'I'd like that very much,' Josh whispered back. 'But only if that's what your mum wants too.'

Stevie didn't bother trying to stop her tears as she joined in the whispered conversation. 'I'd like that very much, too.'

And there it was again. That look of love that Stevie would never get used to seeing.

A look that she knew she could absolutely trust. A love she could trust even more.

'Will you come and live with us then?' Mattie couldn't keep whispering. 'With us and Lucky in our new house?'

The corner of Josh's mouth curled into a smile. 'Do you think it might be better if you all came to live in my house? It's a wee bit bigger.'

'But what about *our* new house?'

'We can talk about that later,' Stevie told him. 'But I'm thinking that if we fixed it up and made it nice, maybe your gran would like to come and live closer to us.'

'Brilliant idea,' Josh agreed.

But Mattie was frowning. 'You said you were scared,' he said slowly. 'And that was why you said you didn't want to be anybody's dad. But you're a grown-up. What are you *scared* of?'

'Ah…' Josh spoke to Mattie as if he was a grown up himself. 'Losing things,' he told him. 'Especially people. This brother that I'm going to tell you all about? His name's Lachlan and…and he's pretty sick right now.'

'Is he going to die?'

Stevie lifted her arm from around Mattie

to touch Josh as she saw him struggling to answer. And she filled the silence.

'We hope not,' she said. 'There's a special way that Josh might be able to help him get better. It's called a stem cell transplant but Josh can tell you all about that. He needs to talk to Lachlan about it first.'

'Yeah… I do.' Josh got to his feet. 'And there's no time like the present, is there? I reckon he's going to be really happy to hear that Mattie's going to have a dad because—' he was grinning at Mattie '—that means he's going to be an uncle, doesn't it?'

Mattie's eyes widened. 'He hasn't even met me.'

'So come with me.'

'Oh…' Stevie got to her feet. 'But it's you that Lachlan needs to see now. It's a private sort of family conversation you need to have.'

'Exactly.' Josh held out his hand. 'And you're family, too. *My* family.'

Stevie took hold of Josh's hand and took a step forward.

'Wait for me.' Mattie scooped Lucky into his arms as he jumped to his feet. 'I'm coming, too.'

The shared glance between Stevie and Josh was full of laughter this time. As if they'd leave him behind… He'd brought them together in the first place and somehow he'd created the space that had convinced them both that they could trust what they had together. For ever.

They all went towards the car. They had an important visit to make now and Stevie knew it was a big step into her future and, whatever that future held, if they were together it was all she could ever have hoped for.

Stevie made sure Mattie had clicked his seat belt into place in the back seat as Josh instructed Lucky to lie down on his blanket. She turned to get into the front seat but Josh caught her shoulder to turn her and then pulled her into his arms. He caught her gaze first.

'I love you,' he said softly.

'I know.' Stevie wanted to smile but this was too big. 'I love you, too…'

Josh caught her lips, then, in the softest, most eloquent kiss in the world. So tender it broke Stevie's heart—in a very good way…

'Ew…that's so gross…' Mattie had his face pressed against the window. 'Can we go now?'

They both laughed but then Josh touched her lips again with the briefest promise of a kiss. And then they caught each other's gaze and both spoke at exactly the same time. Whispered, in fact, so Mattie couldn't hear.

'Later...'

* * * * *

*Look out for the next story in the Twins
Reunited on the Children's Ward duet*

A Surgeon with a Secret

*And if you enjoyed this story, check
out these other great reads from
Alison Roberts*

**Falling for the Secret Prince
The Paramedic's Unexpected Hero
Saved by Their Miracle Baby**

All available now!